TRANSLATOR'S NOTE

Until 2010, Japan had a fifteen-year statute of limitations on the crime of murder.

PENANCE

ALSO BY KANAE MINATO

Confessions

PENANCE

Kanae Minato

Translated by Philip Gabriel

MULHOLLAND BOOKS

Little, Brown and Company
New York Boston London

Mulholland Books / Little, Brown and Company
Hachette Book Group
1290 Avenue of the Americas, New York, NY 10104
mulhollandbooks.com

First English language edition, April 2017
Originally published in Japan as *Shokuzai* by Futabasha Publishers Ltd., Tokyo, 2012
English translation rights arranged with Futabasha Publishers Ltd. through Japan UNI Agency, Inc., Tokyo.

Mulholland Books is an imprint of Little, Brown and Company, a division of Hachette Book Group, Inc. The Mulholland Books name and logo are trademarks of Hachette Book Group, Inc.

The publisher is not responsible for websites (or their content) that are not owned by the publisher.

The Hachette Speakers Bureau provides a wide range of authors for speaking events. To find out more, go to hachettespeakersbureau.com or call (866) 376-6591.

Library of Congress Cataloging-in-Publication Data
Names: Minato, Kanae, author. | Gabriel, Philip, translator.
Title: Penance / Kanae Minato; translated by Philip Gabriel.
Other titles: Kyōgū. English
Description: First English language edition. | New York: Mulholland Books/Little, Brown and Company, 2017.
Identifiers: LCCN 2016038359 | ISBN 978-0-316-34915-4 (paperback)
Subjects: LCSH: Girls—Crimes against—Fiction. | Young women—Fiction. | Revenge—Fiction. | BISAC: FICTION / Mystery & Detective / Women Sleuths. | GSAFD: Mystery fiction.
Classification: LCC PL873.I535 A2 2017 | DDC 895.63/6—dc23
LC record available at https://lccn.loc.gov/2016038359

10 9 8 7 6 5 4 3 2 1

LSC-C

Printed in the United States of America

CONTENTS

PENANCE

French Doll

Dear Asako,

Thank you so much for attending my wedding the other day.

I was worried all through the ceremony that when you saw the crowd of my relatives who'd come from that country town you'd remember the events that took place back then, back in that town, and be upset. They never seem aware of how rude they are sometimes.

The only good thing about that town I grew up in is the sparkling clean air. The first time I realized this—that besides the clean air the town had little else to recommend it—was seven years ago, after I'd graduated from high school and gone on to a women's college in Tokyo.

I lived in the college dorm for four years. When I told my parents I wanted to go to Tokyo for college, both of them were dead set against it.

Some lowlife might trick you, they argued, and force you into prostitution. Then what? What'll you do if you get hooked on drugs? Or get killed?

You were raised in the city, Asako, so I'm sure you'll laugh when you read this, wondering what could possibly lead them to these ideas.

"You watch too much *24 City*," I countered, naming one of my parents' favorite TV shows, but the truth is I'd often imagined the same kind of frightening scenario. Still, I desperately wanted to go to Tokyo.

"What's so special about Tokyo?" my father shot back. "There are other colleges in our prefecture that offer the major you're interested in. If it's too much to commute to school from home, apartments are cheaper here. And if anything happens, you can always come home. We can all rest easy."

"Rest easy? Are you kidding? You're the ones who know best how petrified I've been the last eight years living here."

Once I said this, they stopped their objections. They'd allow me to go to Tokyo, but on one condition: that I didn't live alone in an apartment, but in the dorm. I was fine with that.

I'd never been to Tokyo in my life and found it a totally different world. When I got off the Shinkansen train the first time, the station was packed—people as far as the eye could see. There were probably more people in the station alone than in the whole town I'd just come from. But what surprised me even more was how people managed to walk without bumping into each other. Even as I wandered around, stopping to check the signs to take the subway, I was able to arrive at my destination without colliding with anyone.

I was surprised, too, when I got on the subway. Passengers hardly ever talked to each other, even when they'd gotten on board with others. Occasionally I'd hear someone laugh or people talking, but those were usually foreigners, not Japanese.

Until junior high I'd walked to school every day, then ridden a bicycle, so the only time I'd taken a train was a couple of times a year when I went with friends or family to a neighboring town to a department store or shopping mall. During the hour-long ride we never stopped talking.

What should I buy? It's their birthday next month so I should get them something. What should we have for lunch? McDonald's or KFC? ... The way we acted—talking the entire way—wasn't so outlandish, I don't think. There were lots of people talking and laughing throughout the train, and nobody objected, so I always thought that was how you acted on trains.

It suddenly struck me that Tokyo residents don't notice their surroundings. They have no interest in the people around them. As long as the person sitting next to them isn't bothering them, they couldn't care less. Not a speck of interest in the title of the book the person across the aisle from them is reading. Even if the person standing right in front of them is carrying an expensive designer bag, nobody notices.

Before I realized it, I was crying. *People might think I'm homesick*, I thought, *a hick lugging a huge bag around, sitting there blubbering.* Embarrassed, I wiped away the tears, glancing nervously around me, but not a single person was looking at me.

Right then it struck me: Tokyo was a more wonderful place than I'd ever imagined.

I didn't come to Tokyo for the upscale shopping or all the great places to have fun at. What I wanted was to melt into the crowds of people who didn't know about my past, and vanish.

More precisely, because I'd witnessed a murder, and the person who committed it had not been caught, what I wanted more than anything was to disappear from his radar forever.

Four of us shared a dorm room, all from rural places far from Tokyo, and the first day in the dorm we vied with each other in bragging about our hometowns. My place has the most delicious udon noodles, one said proudly, mine has a hot springs, mine has a famous Major League Baseball player who lives near my parents' house, said another. That sort of thing. The other three girls were from the countryside, but at least I'd heard of the towns they came from.

But when I told them the name of my town, none of them even knew which prefecture it was in.

"What kind of place is it?" they asked, and I answered: "A place where the air is sparkling clean." I know you of all people would understand this, Asako, that I wasn't just saying this because I had nothing else to be proud of.

I'd been born in that rural town and breathed the air there every day without ever giving it a second thought. But the first time I became aware that the air was so very pure and fresh was just after I entered fourth grade, the spring of the year the murder took place.

One day our social studies teacher, Ms. Sawada, told us, "You all live in the place with the cleanest air in all of Japan. Do you know why I can say that? Precision instruments used in hospitals and research have to be manufactured in a completely dust-free environment. That's why they build factories that make these instruments in places where the air is pure. And this year a new factory was built here by Adachi Manufacturing Company. That the top precision instrument maker in Japan built a factory here means this town was chosen because it has the cleanest air in the whole country. You should all be very proud of living in this wonderful town."

After class we asked Emily if what the teacher said was true.

"Papa said the same thing," she replied.

That decided it. Since Emily said so, we knew our town really *did* have clean, pure air. We didn't believe it because her father, with his fierce look and glaring eyes, was some higher-up in Adachi Manufacturing. We believed it because he was from Tokyo.

The town didn't have a single mini-mart back then, but none of us kids minded. We accepted things the way they were. We might see commercials on TV for Barbie dolls, but we'd never actually laid eyes on any so we didn't particularly want one. Far more precious to us were the fancy French dolls that people in town proudly displayed in their living rooms.

Still, after the new factory came, a strange new sensation started to arise among us. From Emily and the other transfer students from Tokyo, we started to detect that the lifestyle we'd always thought was perfectly normal was, in fact, inconvenient and behind the times.

Everything about these new residents' lives was different, starting with where they lived. After Adachi Manufacturing came to town, the company built an apartment building for employees, the first building ever in town over five stories tall. It was designed to harmonize with the surroundings, but for us it rose up like a castle in some far-off land.

One day Emily invited some of the girls in her class who lived in the West District part of town, where the building was, to her apartment on the top, the seventh, floor. The night before, I was so excited I couldn't sleep.

Four of us were invited to her place: me, Maki, Yuka, and Akiko, all friends from long ago, raised in the same neighborhood.

When we entered Emily's apartment it felt like stepping into a foreign land. The open floor plan was the first surprise. We had no concept at the time of an LDK—a combined great room type of living-dining-kitchen space—and were surprised that the places where you watched TV and cooked and ate were all a single unit, with no walls separating them.

We were served English tea in teacups we kids would never have been allowed to touch if they were in our house, with a matching teapot, and on matching plates were tarts with a variety of different fruits I'd never seen before. The strawberries were the only fruit I recognized. I stuffed myself, enraptured, but felt as if something wasn't quite right.

After eating we decided to play dolls and Emily brought out a Barbie doll and a plastic, heart-shaped dress case from her room. The Barbie doll was dressed exactly as Emily was that day.

"There's a shop in Shibuya that sells the same outfits that Barbie wears, and my parents bought it for me for my birthday last year. Right, Mama?"

All I wanted at this point was to get out of there.

Right then one of the other girls said, "Emily, could you show us your family's French doll?"

"What's that?" Emily shot us a blank stare.

Emily didn't own a French doll. And she had no idea what we were talking about. I'd been feeling deflated, but hearing this, I perked up. It was only natural that Emily didn't know about French dolls. In the city they were an obsolete status symbol.

The old Japanese-style wooden homes around our town all had one thing in common. The room closest to the front door, a sitting room, was done in Western style and was sure to have a chandelier and a French doll inside a glass display case. People had owned French dolls for ages, but about a month before Emily moved to town it suddenly became popular for the local girls to go from house to house to admire the different dolls.

At first we just went to friends' houses, but soon we started dropping by other people's houses in the neighborhood. It was a rural town and we knew almost everyone by sight, and the room was right next to the entrance, so hardly anybody turned us down.

Before long we began compiling Doll Memos, as we called them, ranking the French dolls we'd seen. Back then kids couldn't snap photos easily like now, so we drew pictures of the dolls in notebooks with colored pencils.

Mostly we ranked them according to how pretty the dresses

were, but I liked looking at the dolls' faces. I felt as if the dolls people chose reflected their personalities, and the faces of the dolls seemed to resemble the faces of the mother and kids in the family.

Emily said she wanted to see some French dolls, so we took her on a tour of the ten best in our rankings. Emily was sure that the other children in her building hadn't seen French dolls before either, so she invited a few to join her and we all trooped off to various homes in town along with children whose grades and names we didn't even know. For some reason a few boys tagged along, too.

The person in the first house we visited said, "Oh, so you're on the French Doll Tour?" We liked the term so much, that's what we dubbed our outing that day.

The French doll in my house was ranked number two on the list. The neckline and hem of the pink dress were fringed with soft, pure-white feathers, with large purple roses adorning the shoulders and waist. But what I really liked was how the doll's face looked a bit like mine. I'd added a small mole under the right eye, like I have, with Magic Marker, which upset my mother. I also liked that it wasn't clear how old the doll was supposed to be, whether it was a child or an adult.

"Isn't it great?" I boasted, but the city kids had already lost interest, and I remember being bitterly disappointed.

After we'd visited the last home Emily said, "I guess I like Barbie dolls better after all." I think she said it innocently enough, but that one statement from her was all it took for those French dolls, up till now the most radiant things in our lives, to suddenly appear worthless. After that day we stopped playing with French dolls, and my Doll Memo disappeared into the back of a drawer.

But three months later the words *French doll* were on everyone's lips in town, because of the so-called French Doll Robbery. I wonder how much you know about this incident, Asako.

At the end of July, on the evening of the summer festival, French dolls were stolen from five houses in town, my house included. There was no other damage to the houses, and no money stolen. Just the French dolls missing from their glass display cases. A strange affair all around.

The festival was held on the grounds of the civic center on the outskirts of town, with the Obon dances starting around 6 p.m., a karaoke contest at 9, and then the whole event winding up at 11 p.m. The neighborhood association provided watermelons, ice cream, somen noodles, and beer free of charge, and there were a few stalls selling shaved ice and cotton candy. It was a big event for the town.

The homes the French dolls were stolen from, including mine, had two things in common. First, the whole family was out at the festival, and second, none of the houses had locked their front doors. Most houses in town were like that at the time, I think. When people were asked to deliver something to another house, they would just open the front door when no one was at home and place the package inside. It's just what people did.

Since we'd had our little French Doll Tour, the police right away pegged it as a prank by children, but the perpetrator and the dolls were never found, and eventually it was shelved as some unexplained, odd event on the night of the festival.

I remember my father getting angry with me: "It's because you kids had that tour, that's why. Some child who didn't have a French doll at home got jealous and stole them."

Our summer vacation started with that incident, but still we went out every day, from morning to evening, to play. We especially liked the pool at our elementary school. We'd spend the morning at one of our houses doing our summer homework assignments, then go to the pool in the afternoon, and even after the pool closed at four we'd stick around the school grounds playing until it got dark.

Nowadays even rural elementary schools have put in place various crime prevention measures, not allowing anyone, even kids, onto the grounds on days when there's no school, but back then we could play until dark and no one said a word.

Sometimes, even, if we went back home before "Greensleeves" started playing over the town PA system, announcing that it was 6 p.m., our parents would ask what was wrong, whether we'd quarreled with our friends.

Right after the murder that day, and many times afterward, I told everything, all I could possibly recall about it, to the police, to teachers at school, to my parents, to the parents of the other children, and to you, Asako, and your husband. But here I'd like to write down the events one more time, in the order they occurred. For what will probably be the very last time...

On that day, the evening of August fourteenth, a lot of the kids we usually played with had gone to relatives' houses for the

Obon holiday, or had relatives visiting theirs, so it was just five of us playing in the school grounds—me, Maki, Yuka and Akiko, and Emily.

The four of us from town either lived with our grandparents, or our grandparents and relatives lived in town, so Obon wasn't a particularly special day for us and we went out to play like always.

Most of the people from the Adachi factory who'd moved here from Tokyo were out of town for the holiday. Emily, though, was still in town because her father worked through the holiday, she told us that day. Later, at the end of August, they were going to take a family vacation to Guam.

The French Doll Tour had introduced a little awkwardness into our relationship with Emily, but that soon passed and we were all friends again. One reason may have been Emily's enthusiasm for playing Explorers, which was popular then.

The pool was closed through the Obon holiday, so we played volleyball in a corner of the school grounds, in the shade next to the gym. All we did was form a circle and pass the ball back and forth, but we were really into it, aiming to pass the ball a hundred times without missing.

That's when that man appeared.

"Hello there, do you girls have a second?" we heard a voice ask.

A gray work shirt with yellowish-green tinge, work pants, a white towel wrapped around his head.

The sudden voice threw Yuka, who was out of form that day, and she missed a pass. The man picked up the ball, which had rolled toward him, and came over to us. Smiling broadly, he said the following quite clearly:

"I'm here to check the ventilation fan for the changing rooms in the pool, but I totally forgot to bring a ladder. We just need to tighten a few screws, so could one of you ride piggy-back on my shoulders and help out?"

Nowadays elementary school pupils would have been on their guard in a situation like this. Schools are not necessarily seen as safe places. If we had been aware of that, I wonder if we would have avoided what happened. Maybe we should have been taught to scream and run away if a stranger talked to us?

In our small, rural town, though, the most we'd been warned was not to get in a stranger's car if he told us he'd give us gum or candy, or told us our parents were sick and he'd take us to them.

So we weren't at all suspicious about this man before us. I don't know about Emily, but I think that's how the others felt. In fact, when we heard the words *help out* we vied to be the one chosen.

"I'm the smallest, so you could piggyback me easiest," one of us said.

"But what if you can't reach the fan? Shouldn't I go since I'm the tallest?"

"But can either of you tighten screws? I'm good at it."

"What if the screws are hard to turn? I'm really strong, so I think I should do it."

Those are the sorts of things we said, I think. Emily didn't say a thing. As if sizing us up, the man looked from one to the other.

"Can't be too small or too big...," he said. "And if your glasses fall off, that's no good. And you might be a bit too heavy...."

Lastly he turned to Emily.

"You're just right," he said.

Emily glanced at us with a slightly worried look. Maki, perhaps disappointed that Emily had beaten her out, suggested we all help. Good idea, the three of us agreed.

"Thanks," the man said, "but the changing room is kind of small and if everyone comes it'll be hard to work, and I don't want anyone to get hurt. So could you all stay here? It won't take long. I'll buy you all ice cream afterward."

How could we object to that? "Okay, then," the man said, took Emily by the hand, and led her across the school grounds. The pool was beyond the spacious grounds, and we went back to playing volleyball before the two of them had disappeared.

We played for a while, then sat down in the cool shade of the steps at the entrance to the gym and chatted. They're not taking me anywhere for summer vacation. I wish my grandpa's house were a little farther away. Emily's going to Guam next week. Is Guam part of America? Or a country called Guam? I don't know....Emily's so lucky. She has on a Barbie dress today, too. Her face is so pretty, too. You call those kind of eyes almond eyes, right? She looks so cool. And her father and mother look like goggle-eyed aliens. Her miniskirt is so cute. Emily has such long legs. Oh, did you hear? Emily's already started *that*. What do you mean—*that*? Sae, you really don't know?

That was the first time I'd ever heard the word *menstruate*.

The girls in school were assembled to hear about this the year after, in fifth grade, and my mother hadn't talked to me about it yet. I didn't have an older sister or any older girls among my relatives, so I was clueless about what they were talking about.

The other three either had older sisters or else their moms had told them about it, and they began explaining it to me as if displaying some astounding knowledge.

Menstruation is proof that your body's able to have babies, they said. Blood drips out from between your legs. Huh? Are you saying Emily's able to have a baby? That's right. Your older sister, too, Yuka? That's right. I'll probably start mine soon so Mom bought me some underwear for that. What? You, too, Maki? Girls who are big start in fifth grade, they say. But you, Sae, you won't start till junior high. By high school everybody has it, they say. You've got to be kidding. I mean, no junior high girls have babies. That's because they didn't make them. Make them? Sae, are you saying you don't know where babies come from? Oh, yeah—when they get married. Honestly! Girls do dirty things with boys, that's how.

I hope all this stupid stuff I'm writing won't make you rip this letter up.

Caught up in our conversation, we suddenly noticed that "Greensleeves" was playing, the signal it was 6 p.m.

"My older cousin's coming over with his friend today so they told me to come home by six," Akiko said. It being Obon, we decided it best to all go home early, and we went off to fetch Emily. As we crossed the grounds I turned around and saw that the shadows had lengthened considerably since we'd been playing volleyball. I suddenly realized how much time had passed since Emily had gone, and grew concerned.

The pool was surrounded with a wire mesh fence but the gate was unlocked, just shut with a wire. I think until that year it was always like that in the summer.

From the gate you walked up some stairs and there was the pool, with two prefab buildings, changing rooms, beyond. The one on the right was for boys, the left for girls. As we walked next to the pool I thought how very quiet it was.

The changing rooms had sliding doors, and of course were also unlocked. Maki, in front, was the one who opened the girls' room.

"Emily—are you finished?" she called out as she slid open the door. "Huh?" she said, tilting her head. No one was inside.

"I wonder if they finished and she went home," Akiko said.

"Then what about the ice cream? Maybe he only bought Emily some," Yuka said, peeved.

"That's not fair," Maki added.

"What about this one?" I pointed to the boys' changing room, but there was no sound from inside.

"She's not there. There're no voices. See?"

It was Akiko, still facing us, who reluctantly slid open the door to the boys' changing room. The other three of us held our breath. *"Wh—?"* Akiko said, turning around and then letting out a scream.

Emily, head pointed toward the entrance, lay on the drainboards in the middle of the floor.

"Emily?" Maki ventured fearfully. Then all of us called out her name. But Emily lay there, unmoving, eyes wide open.

"Oh my God!" Maki shouted. If at that moment she'd said "She's dead!" we might have been so terrified that we'd have dashed right home.

"We have to tell people," Maki said. "Akiko, you're the fastest runner, so run to Emily's house. Yuka, you go to the police station. I'll look for a teacher. Sae, you keep watch here."

As soon as Maki told us what to do, the others ran off. That was the last time the four of us acted together. I don't think what I've said differs much from the testimony the other three gave.

The four of us girls were interviewed together many times about what preceded the murder, but we weren't asked in detail about after we found the body. And we haven't talked much with each other about the murder, so I don't know that much about what the others did after this.

What I'm going to tell you now is just what I did.

Alone in the changing room after the other girls left, I looked over again at Emily. She had on a black T-shirt with a pink Barbie logo written across the chest, but the shirt was rolled up so high you could barely make it out. I could see her white stomach and the slight swell of her breasts. Her red checked pleated skirt was rolled up, too, and the bottom half of her body, with no panties on, was exposed.

I was asked to guard her, but I felt like if any adult were to come they'd yell at me for letting her body be exposed like this. "The poor girl!" they'd scold. "Why didn't you cover her up?" I hadn't done this to Emily, yet I felt as if I'd be the one they'd blame. So hesitantly I stepped inside the changing room.

The first thing I did was use my handkerchief to cover up her open eyes and mouth, which had liquid dripping out. And, avoiding looking at Emily, I held the T-shirt with my fingers and rolled it down. There was white, sticky stuff all over her stomach, though at the time I had no idea what it was. I rearranged her skirt, too. As I crouched down I saw her panties, all crumpled up and tossed aside at the lowest row of lockers.

What should I do with her panties? I wondered. I'd been able to rearrange her shirt and skirt without touching her body, but that wouldn't work with her panties. I glanced at Emily's long, white legs, spread apart, and saw blood flowing down her thighs from her crotch.

That's when I got scared and ran out of the changing room.

I think I was able, even realizing she was dead, to rearrange her clothes because she'd been strangled and there wasn't any blood. The second I was out of the changing room, though, the pool in front of me frightened me, and I froze. In a short space of time the sun had gotten really low and the wind had come up. I stared at the tiny ripples on the surface of the pool and felt as if I were going to be dragged in. They say that during Obon—the festival for departed spirits—if you go swimming the dead will grab your leg. Every year I heard this warning, and now it rattled around in my head and I had the sudden illusion that Emily was going to arise and, to take me with her to the land of the dead, push me into the pool. I closed my eyes and crouched down, head in hands to stop up my ears, and kept on shrieking so loud it felt as if my throat would burst.

Why couldn't I lose consciousness? If I could have made

myself faint, the situation I find myself in now might be very different.

I'm not sure how long I stayed like that, but the first one to appear on the scene was you, Asako. I'm sure you remember what happened after that, so here I'll simply write about what happened with me.

Yuka returned with the local patrolman. Then right after that my mother showed up, worried that I hadn't come home and aware that something had happened. She put me on her back and carried me straight home. I cried for the first time after I got home. I think I cried even more loudly then than when I was screaming by the pool.

My mother didn't press me at first about what had happened. As I lay down on some zabuton cushions, she gave me cold barley tea, gently rubbed my back, then murmured, "I'm glad it wasn't you, Sae."

As her voice sank deep into my head I closed my eyes and fell asleep.

What I'm writing here isn't much different from the testimony I gave right after the murder. I think all four of us gave pretty clear testimony, considering the kind of incident we'd witnessed.

Even now, though, I feel regret about the one thing we couldn't say for certain, the one thing none of the four of us could recall.

I can see all that happened that day very clearly in my mind, like images on a TV screen, but for some reason the one thing I can't recall is the man's face.

"The man had a white towel wrapped around his head."

"He was wearing gray work clothes."

"Weren't they a light greenish color?"

"How old was he? He looked like forty, or maybe fifty."

Though we had an overall impression of the man, we never could recall his face. Was he tall or short? Heavy or thin? Was his face round, or more narrow? Were his eyes big or small? What about his nose, his mouth, his eyebrows? Did he have any moles or scars? Even when his appearance was broken down into details like this, all we could do was shake our heads.

One thing, though, was for certain. We'd never seen him before.

For a time the murder was the sole topic of conversation in our small, rural town. Once a relative of mine came by to ask me more about the murder, just out of curiosity, and my mother chased him away. People started talking about the French Doll Robbery and linking the two incidents. Maybe, they said, there's some pervert in our town or nearby who likes young girls. Whoever stole the dolls maybe wasn't satisfied with them and murdered a cute-as-a-doll young girl. People whispered these rumors as if they were entirely plausible.

The police started questioning people in the places the dolls were stolen from again, so almost everyone started to see the two incidents as the work of one criminal, a pervert who liked young girls.

But I wasn't convinced. Because I was the one whose appearance would best be described as that of an *innocent young girl*.

Ever since the murder, if I let my attention wander I start

to visualize Emily's dead body. It's a black-and-white image—only, the blood trickling down her thighs is bright red. And in my mind my face gets superimposed on Emily's and my head starts to ache. And as I hold my throbbing head, one thought runs through my mind.

Thank God it wasn't me.

I'm sure you find this an awful thing to think. I have no idea what the other three girls thought. Some of them might have been so sad for Emily, and some might have been wracked with guilt, wondering why they couldn't have saved her. For me, though, it was all I could do to worry about myself.

What came after *Thank God it wasn't me* was *Why Emily?* And I had a clear answer for that. It was because, of the five of us, she was the only one who'd reached adulthood. It was because she was a grown-up that that man did awful things to her and murdered her.

That man—the murderer—was looking for a young girl who'd just become an adult.

A month passed, then half a year, then a year, and still the criminal hadn't been found. I believe it was three years after the murder that you moved back to Tokyo, Asako. I wonder if you realize I am writing this letter because of the promise we made then.

Time passed, and as people in town spoke less of the murder, the fear grew stronger within me. Even if I didn't remember the murderer's face, he might remember mine. He might think we knew his face and come to murder me and the other girls. Until now adults around us had kept an eye on us, but they were gradually slacking off. Perhaps he was waiting for us to start doing things on our own again, without any adults around....

I had the constant sensation that the murderer was watching me. Through gaps in a window, from the shadows of a building, from inside a car.

I was terrified, absolutely petrified. I didn't want to be killed. And in order not to be, there was one thing I had to avoid at all costs.

I could never grow up.

Still, as time passed, even though I'd occasionally sense someone watching me, the murder faded from my mind a little, too. In junior high and high school I was in the wind instrument ensemble, and the intense practice sessions kept me so busy practicing every day, I had little time to consider the past.

This doesn't mean that I was mentally and physically ever free of the murder. I realized this—was *made* to realize it— when I was seventeen and a junior in high school.

Seventeen years old and I still hadn't had my first period. I might have been small, physically, but that didn't explain why I hadn't started menstruating. Maybe I was still within the acceptable age range for a first period, but my mother suggested I have a doctor examine me, so I went to the gynecological department at the prefectural hospital in the next town over.

It takes a lot of courage for a high school girl to go to an OB-GYN clinic. But I realized that up till then I hadn't given any thought to menstruation, and though I had an idea why this was the case, I imagined that couldn't be the reason I hadn't yet had a period. It would be terrible to have some kind of actual gynecological problem, I thought, so I steeled myself and went.

There was a private OB-GYN clinic in our town, but the last thing I wanted was for people in town to spot me going there. I'd barely talked to any boys, let alone gone out with any, but couldn't stand the thought of ugly rumors flying around. So I went to another town to get checked out.

The tests showed nothing out of the ordinary, and the doctor said it might be psychological. "Are you experiencing any kind of stress at school or at home?" he asked.

When I learned that periods can start, and stop, because of psychological reasons, it made sense. *If I become an adult I'll get killed,* I thought. *If my periods start, I'll get murdered.* I had been suggesting this to my body all along, at first consciously, then gradually unconsciously. Even if I didn't consciously think of the murder very often, it had still been constantly at work in the deeper recesses of my mind.

The hospital recommended counseling and regular hormone injections, and I said I'd talk it over with my parents. That was the last time I went to the hospital. I reported back to my mother that they'd found nothing wrong and that I was just a little late.

I was praying even more now that my period wouldn't start before the statute of limitations on the murder ran out.

Even if I left the town, got lost in the crowds in Tokyo, and lived among people who knew nothing of the murder, who knew but that I might run across the murderer again? But my body, still not that of an adult, would keep me from harm. That's the sense of security I sought.

I didn't hope so much that the murderer would be arrested, and the murder brought up all over again, but more that the statute of limitations would come quickly and I would finally be freed from the past.

This had nothing to do with the promise I made to you, Asako.

Still, I never dreamed I would ever see you again.

After graduating from a women's college with an English degree, I was hired by a medium-size company that mainly dealt with dyes. Whether you'd graduated in the sciences or the humanities, all new employees spent the first two years assigned to the laboratory. They did this to teach us what kinds of products the company was dealing in.

This was the first time since high school chemistry class that I'd touched test tubes and beakers, and the first time I'd ever seen one of those analysis devices that cost tens of millions of yen. Gas chromatography, liquid chromatography—they explained what these square, boxy devices did, but it flew right over my head. But the company logo on the side of the machines did catch my eye.

Adachi Manufacturing. So these were made at the factory back in my hometown with its pure, clean air, I realized, and felt a sudden closeness to them. At the same time, a sense of disgust welled up, as if that town had been lying in wait for me. This complex mix of emotions stayed with me starting shortly after I was hired.

It was in the spring at the beginning of my third year in the company that the head of the laboratory approached me about a possible marriage candidate. This was right after I'd finished my two-year stint in the lab and had officially been assigned to the accounting department.

"He's the son of a cousin of the managing director of one of our top clients. He saw you somewhere and asked to be formally introduced."

If the head of the lab had spoken to me privately about this, I probably would have turned him down, even though it was one of the company executives asking. I wasn't, after all, someone who could consider getting married. But he asked me—loudly—in front of my coworkers, just as all of us who'd joined the company at the same time were gathering our belongings in the lab in preparation for moving to the various departments to which we'd been assigned. He handed me the man's photograph and personal history right then and there, and my coworkers crowded around, dying of curiosity.

I opened the folder with the photo of the man, and some of the other women voiced their approval—"Looking good!" When I looked at the man's CV the men in the lab voiced theirs, too: "Impressive!" Seeing their reaction, the head of the lab said, "What do you think? Pretty amazing, eh?" egging them on. "He's quite a catch for you," some of my colleagues said. "This is your big chance!" I'd completely lost the opportunity to turn him down flat and ended up replying that I'd be happy to meet the man.

But why would an elite man like that, a graduate of a top university working in a top corporation, and a stylish-looking guy, ask to meet someone like me, a nothing office worker in a third-rate company, and think I might be a suitable marriage partner? What was I doing when he spotted me and got interested? Thoughts like these ran through my head over and over before the day of our first meeting, and I arrived at one conclusion: he must be mistaking me for someone else.

We avoided the usual stiff *omiai* meeting with go-betweens present and instead arranged for just the two of us to have dinner. But actually that made me feel depressed. I was earning my own living now and finally able to talk with men like everyone else, but I'd never had dinner alone with a man I'd just met.

I was wearing a springlike pink dress recommended by one of the busybody women hired at the same time as me. I arrived at the hotel lobby where we were to meet and soon after, a man came up, the same one in the photograph. This was Takahiro.

Very cheerfully and politely he apologized for asking my boss to set things up, and thanked me for coming on my day off. I floundered a bit, unable to get out a decent reply. We went up to the Italian restaurant on the top floor, and after settling in I handed him a copy of my own CV, unimpressive as it was.

But he set it on a corner of the table without a glance.

"You grew up in —— Town, didn't you?" he asked.

I gulped when he mentioned the name of that town, the one with the pure, clean air. He went on, a smile on his face.

"I lived in that town too, for three years, from sixth grade in elementary school to the second year of junior high. We were two years apart in school, so I don't imagine you remember me."

Remember? How could I when I didn't even know him? If

he'd been in sixth grade that meant I had been in fourth. That was the year the factory was built and the school was suddenly crawling with transfer students.

"I'm sorry you don't remember," he said. "But we played together once. The French Doll Tour. You were the one in charge and took us to see all the dolls."

Ah—so he was in that group. Still, I couldn't recall which child he had been. But he changed the subject before I could relive the sense of defeat I'd had then, and before I could think much about the French Doll Robbery. He lived in the town three years, so naturally he knew about the robbery, perhaps even knew I'd been caught up in it. Maybe he was avoiding the topic out of consideration for me.

Takahiro worked in sales, in a division dealing with watches, so he had many opportunities to visit Switzerland, and as he was reminiscing about my hometown one day, how it reminded him a bit of Switzerland, he'd happened to catch sight of me again and had wanted to meet me.

"Where was this?" I asked, and he said it was at what he imagined was my company's end-of-year party. I mentioned the name of a Chinese restaurant. "Yes!" he said. "That's the place. I was there with a friend," he said, "next to you, and thought, *Do coincidences like this really happen?*" He was even a little embarrassed, he said, wondering if it was fate that had brought us together again. Now, though, I see that he was just saying whatever came into his head.

After that Takahiro and I saw each other once or twice a week. We'd have dinner, or go to a movie or art museum, typical date scenarios, but strangely, when I was with him I felt free from the fear that someone was watching me. So much so that each time we said goodbye I wanted to stay with him a little longer.

But he never asked me to go to a hotel with him, or said he wanted to come up to my apartment, where I lived alone. And of course when he took me back to my building by taxi I never invited him in for a coffee or anything. If I had, and he had come to my place, what then? Whose voice was this in my head, wondering this?

It was on our seventh date that he suddenly proposed.

This was the first time we held hands. Nothing particularly romantic about it—we'd gone to the opening performance of a famous musical and he held on to my hand so we wouldn't get separated in the crowded lobby—but that was enough to set my heart pounding. Later, after we were seated in the darkened theater, I was overwhelmed with sadness and even shed a few tears.

"I've been assigned long-term to Switzerland and hoped you could come with me."

Takahiro proposed at dinner, after we had been served a fancy French-*kaiseki* dessert and accompanying wine. The restaurant was very private, each table in its own individual room, the perfect place for a marriage proposal. It felt like a dream, and I thought how happy I would be if I could accept it openly, without any reservations.

But I couldn't. And there was a reason why.

"I'm very sorry," I said, bowing to him, "but I can't accept."

"Why not?" he asked. The proposal wasn't totally unexpected, but it had me flustered. I wished I could have turned him down by giving some typical, trite reason, telling him he should find someone who would be more suitable for him instead of settling for a nobody like me. But this would have been a lie. So I went ahead and revealed the real reason.

I never imagined I would reveal that loathsome truth about me as a reply to a marriage proposal.

"I'm defective, as a woman."

He looked flabbergasted. I'm sure he never expected to hear that. Before I was overcome by shame, I got the whole thing out.

"Even now," I said, "at age twenty-five, I've never had a period, not even once. Because deep down inside me I'm rejecting the idea of my body becoming a woman's. A body like that can't have normal sexual relations, or have a child. A man like you, with a wonderful future ahead of him, shouldn't marry some defective article like me."

For the first time I cursed the way my mind had tricked my body in order to protect me. *If this is how things were going to turn out,* I thought with regret, *I should have done whatever it took—shots or counseling—back when I was a junior in high school.*

I felt it was cowardly to cry, so I held my tears back. I took a bite of the dessert, which was like a piece of fine china, white mousse with a variety of colored berries on top. Strawberries, raspberries, cranberries, blueberries...Since the time I first learned all those different names, that country town had held me in its grasp.

"That doesn't matter," Takahiro said. "If you just come with me, that's fine. If you're there when I come home, tired from work, that's all I need. I'll tell you all that happened that day, and hold you and go to sleep. I can't imagine anything happier than that. Won't you come with me, and start a new life in a place like the one we used to live in together?

"Leaving Japan wouldn't be a bad idea for you," he added. "You probably got like that because of the murder, and maybe you're worried that being in a town that reminds you of your hometown will make you remember all that happened there. But there is one thing I can guarantee.

"In this new place there is no murderer.

"And I will be there to protect you."

I was surprised when Takahiro asked if it was all right to invite you, Asako, and your husband to our wedding. That was the first time I learned that Takahiro's father and your husband were cousins. "When Asako and her husband see me," I asked him, "won't they remember the murder and suffer those terrible memories all over again?" But he said you'd told him you really wanted to attend.

To be perfectly honest, I didn't want to see you again, Asako. I was afraid you would never forgive me for not keeping my promise to you and instead seeking out my own happiness. But I had no right to say anything when it came to the wedding. It was Takahiro's family, after all—both parents were executives with Adachi Manufacturing—who were footing the bill for this extravagant affair, held in an art museum designed by a famous architect, a place where several celebrities had also had their weddings. The only thing I was left to choose by myself was the wedding dress.

But on the day of the wedding you told me, Asako, to forget the murder and be happy. I can't tell you how overjoyed I was when you said that....And one other thing made me really happy that day: the surprise that Takahiro had in store.

When Takahiro and I had been planning the wedding I was sure that, for my midreception change of outfits, I would change into a cocktail dress, but he simply dismissed the idea, urging me to stay in the white wedding dress to the end. The reason became clear during the reception when he suddenly handed me a box with a large ribbon on it and I was led to a waiting room by one of the staff.

I opened the box and found a pink dress inside. The décolleté and hem were edged with white feathers, the shoulders and waist decorated with large purple roses. A matching headband of purple roses and white feathers was also placed on my head. My French doll might wear this kind of headband, I recalled. I looked in the mirror and what I saw was the French doll we used to have in the sitting room of our old house.

But why? I wondered, and then remembered that the first time Takahiro and I met was during the French Doll Tour. Me, a country girl, proudly showing kids from the big city our antique-looking dolls. He must have remembered how I was then, and ordered a dress identical to my doll's. To surprise me, and make me happy.

When I went back into the reception hall Takahiro gazed at me, as if holding his breath, and then burst out in a big smile. "You're gorgeous!" he said.

Everyone kidded us, and toasted us, and two days after this

blissful time, I set off with Takahiro on our trip. From the airplane I watched the scenery on the ground recede and my whole body was filled with a sense of liberation.

In this new place there is no murderer. And I will be there to protect you.

But there *was* a criminal.

The town I'm in now does have clean, fresh air like that other town—that much is true—but other than that there's nothing at all the same. This town is so charming and beautiful. Two weeks have passed since we began our life together, just the two of us.

Hard to believe it's only been two weeks.

I was a little surprised as I wrote this. Up till now I was able to write calmly about things, but I'm not at all sure I can write about the rest as well. But what I'm going to say now is what I really need to write.

I'll start with the day we arrived in this town....

Takahiro had told me that our new house had almost everything we needed in the way of furniture, dishes, and so on, so I'd gotten rid of most of what I had when I lived alone, and had only sent ahead a bare minimum of clothes and other personal items. After we were engaged, Takahiro had gone to Switzerland a number of times on business and had gotten the house ready for us then.

We arrived at the local airport in the morning, and several people from his company came to meet us. I went with Takahiro to his office to meet his colleagues. We all had a meal together to introduce me to everyone, and were even given a lovely wedding present. Then we drove to our new home, just the two of us, in a car provided by his company.

I marveled at everything I saw that day, but I gasped in joy when we arrived at our upscale neighborhood and saw our house, which was like an antique dollhouse.

The house was two stories, with a spacious living room, dining room, and kitchen combination on the first floor, as well as two other rooms. The living room had a sofa set and bookcase, and I went ahead and displayed the heavy standing clock we'd been given as a present. But overall the room was a bit bare. There were enough dishes and utensils in the kitchen, though I thought it would be nice to have a pair of matching cups for us. "An orange tablecloth would look nice on the dining table," I commented. "And I'd love to display lots of photos near the bay window," I added excitedly. Takahiro smiled and told me to go ahead and decorate it any way I liked. "But first," he said, "let's unpack." The boxes we'd sent from Japan were randomly stacked in one of the first-floor rooms.

On the second floor there were four rooms, all of different sizes. "The largest room in the back is the bedroom," he told me, "the others you can use any way you'd like." I looked into each of them in order, starting with the closest. *This place is too big for just the two of us,* I was thinking as I continued down the wide hallway and put my hand on the doorknob of the room in back.

"Let's leave this room for later," Takahiro told me. "I got everything in this one room ready when I was here before, so let's go eat first." His words, and my own shyness over the bedroom being ready for us, kept me from opening the door. I went with him to a nearby restaurant instead.

We had beer and some simple but delicious local dishes, and when we arrived home in high spirits Takahiro suddenly swept me up into his arms, lifted me over the threshold like a princess, and began carrying me up the stairs. We continued down the hallway, and he opened the door of the backmost room, and inside gently lowered me in the middle of the room. The room was pitch-dark but I knew he'd let me down on a bed.

He unzipped my dress and it fell off my shoulders. Right after our wedding we'd stayed at a hotel in Japan for a few days, but Takahiro had been so busy with work, preparing for his new job, that nothing took place between us. But now, I knew, the time had come. Even with my incomplete body I thought my love for him would let me be able to do it. Somehow he'd be able to manage.

My heart was pounding and I was holding my breath when suddenly something came down gently over my head. My arms were slowly put through sleeves, a fastener on the back was zipped up, he held my hand, and I got to my feet as he carefully arranged the bottom of the long dress. I realized he'd put another dress on me.

A light came on in the room. Takahiro had turned on one of the lamps. At that instant what struck me was a vision of a French doll. What smiled back at me from above the beautifully carved wooden table next to the bed was the very face of one of those French dolls displayed in the sitting rooms in that country town.

So he'd bought the exact same kind of doll for me? But that wasn't it. There was a tiny mole beneath the doll's right eye, but the dress was different. It wasn't pink, but light blue. And the dress he'd put on me was an identical light blue dress.

In a daze I turned around to find Takahiro gazing at me with the same smile he'd had at our wedding ceremony.

"My precious doll," he said.

"What the—?" As soon as I got these words out, my voice husky, an angry voice shouted *"Don't speak!"* His smile was replaced by a nervous, irritated look, and for the first time I remembered which child he was back on the French Doll Tour.

Unsure what was going on, not allowed to say a word, I stood there, frozen. His usual cheerful expression quickly returned, and he had me sit on the bed and sat down beside me.

"I'm sorry I shouted. Did it frighten you?" His tone was gentle, but I couldn't reply. He was looking at me, but those weren't the eyes of someone looking at an actual, living person. I gazed back in silence. "You're a good little girl, aren't you," he said, patting my head with his large hand.

And he began to tell his story.

"Until then, I'd never been in love," he said. "All the girls around me were trained since childhood to be well-mannered, to live up to their elite status, but they were conceited, stupid creatures, the lot of them. My mother was no different, complaining constantly about the researchers she supervised, all of them incompetent, according to her, and about my father, who worked in the same department.

"And then we had to move. I couldn't believe that town was even part of Japan, it was so devoid of anything. I'd never seen kids like that before—uncouth and vulgar, so full of jealousy. When I thought I'd have to spend the next few years with them, I felt as if I'd go insane.

"Around this time one of the other children who lived in our building invited me to go see something *interesting,* as she put it. I had no clue it was going to be dolls, but there was nothing better to do, so I went with these grubby little country kids. They would open other people's front doors without knocking, call out 'We'd like to see your doll!' and the people who lived there would yell back 'Go right ahead!' and not even show their faces. The kids would just swarm into people's houses to see what was displayed there. Unbelievable.

"Still, it did turn out to be kind of interesting. Looking at all the things displayed there—not just the dolls but the paintings, certificates, and souvenirs—I painted a mental picture of the kind of people who lived in each house. And sure enough, when the people emerged with drinks for us, barley tea or Calpis, they were just like I'd imagined. I was amazed. Around the fourth house I realized that the dolls resembled the kids in that family, and I started to pay more attention to them. They looked strong-willed, or stuck-up, or none too bright—all the impressions I got were pretty negative.

"I think the second-to-last house we visited was yours. By then I was tired of it all and was thinking to quietly slip away, but the moment I laid eyes on the doll in your house, I knew I had to have it.

"This doll had an unusual face—it was hard to say if it

was more a precocious-looking child or a childlike adult—and I longed to reach out and touch that face and the lithe arms and legs. It was all so charming. *How wonderful it would be,* I thought, *to have this doll always by my side and be able to talk to it.* I had some hopes for the girl who owned the doll, too, but she was a typical shabby specimen, the only resemblance the mole she had in the same spot as the doll.

"Even after I got home I couldn't get that doll out of my mind. Whenever I heard my parents arguing in the next room, I'd think of that doll. When my classmates laughed at me for not knowing the rules to Kick the Can, the doll would come to mind. And finally I made up my mind. I had to have it for myself.

"People let down their guard on festival day even more than usual, so stealing the doll was easy. I took it back home, and did the same for the other four. I took the others so if people found out I was the thief they wouldn't know I was in love with that one particular doll. I tossed the other dolls into the factory incinerator that same day.

"I didn't have a guilty conscience. I was confident I could take better care of you than anyone else.

"Soon after this, that murder took place. What surprised me more than the murder itself was how everyone tried to link the murder and the theft of the dolls.

No way, I thought, *they can't mistake me for a murderer!* I went to see one of the children involved in the murder to check things out for myself. That was your house. The child I went to see was on her way back from school or the police, eyes down as she walked, accompanied by her mother. For just an instant my eyes met the girl's. That instant sent a chill through me. She had the same exact eyes as *you*.

"I'd thought the girl was just some grubby country child, but this could turn into something really amazing, I thought. You, at less than a meter tall, were so wonderful, but imagine a life-size version. That would be even more amazing. I could do more than just talk with you as you stood there—I could have you sit, walk with you, hold you while I go to sleep. I had a premonition that someday a miracle was going to happen.

"Soon reports in the paper said the suspect in the murder was a man in his forties or fifties, and I forgot all about it. All I could think of was you.

"You didn't seem to notice it, but I was always looking at you. At school, on the road home, even in front of your home. Not long after this my parents were reassigned to Tokyo and we moved back there, but each holiday I'd come back to town to see how you were, pretending I wanted to visit the home of one of the more decent kids who lived in that town.

"You grew up just as I had hoped. There was a time when I was worried what would happen if you became impure enough to flirt with men, but you showed no signs of that. When I was in college I thought once of talking to you, but waited patiently, laying the groundwork to make you mine.

"'*I'm defective, as a woman.*' When I heard this it sent a greater thrill through me, greater than back when our eyes first met. Because I knew then you really *were* a genuine, living doll. If it was the murder that made my ideal come to life, then I had the murderer to thank.

"Come here beside me. At nighttime you're my doll."

*   *   *

Perhaps tired out from the trip, or from the long tale, he soon fell asleep, holding me gently. I was still in the dress he'd put on me, as if I really were a precious doll.

Creepy, disgusted...It's impossible to express what I felt then. I realized now that the feeling I had felt for a long time that someone was watching me hadn't just been my imagination. But knowing that it wasn't the murderer didn't give me any sense of relief. Instead, I was struck by the fear that now I was in the grip of something even more bizarre, and that night I didn't sleep a wink. *Tomorrow I'm going back to Japan.* That's all I could think about.

But at dawn, when I silently slipped out of bed, Takahiro didn't try to stop me, though I'm sure he noticed. I took a shower, changed into ordinary clothes, and made a simple breakfast with the bread and eggs we'd bought the day before. By this time he was already up as usual.

"I have to go to work starting today," he said in his usual cheerful way, "but if you get lonely or any problems come up, call my cell phone anytime." He kissed me goodbye and headed to the office.

Maybe last night was all a dream? No—it had really happened. But maybe he'd had too much beer and had been drunk. Maybe he really did like the doll and had actually stolen it, and came up with that story to hide his embarrassment.

Trying to convince myself this had to be the case, I went into our bedroom to start cleaning up and saw the doll there, waiting for me with its usual gentle expression. It had a red dress on now. In the room there were a bed and a table and a wardrobe, the latter two with matching carvings. I slowly approached the wardrobe and yanked the double-hinged doors open wide. Inside were matching dresses in many colors, ones for the doll, and ones for me.

I flinched again and tears welled up. But gradually a smile came to my face. Last night, in the dark, it was frightening to suddenly be made to wear that dress and hear Takahiro's bizarre story, but in the light of day the rows of dresses in the closet appeared gaudy and fun, though ultimately ridiculous. Like clothes a circus clown might wear.

Where did he buy all these clothes, and what was running through his mind when he did? I wondered. Surely he didn't take along pictures of the dresses done in colored pencil to a store, did he? Like the Doll Memo book I'd thrown away long ago?

Back when he was a child, there must have been something missing from his life. Something vital. And the doll in our sitting room, something we might very well have tossed out a few years later, compensated for what he lacked. And now I'm the one who plays that role for him, for a few hours each day. He's the one who brought me from my small, rural town to this far-off place. In order for two imperfect, damaged people to live, what's needed is an absurd ceremony that allows them to hide their imperfections.

I was always good at convincing myself of things.

In the evening when Takahiro returned from work and saw I had on the same ordinary clothes I'd had on in the morning, he looked displeased. So before he could say anything, I got out the following in a rush of words:

"This is, even at night, a space for us to live in, as human beings," I told him. "We'll eat, use the restroom, take a shower, and then won't you spend a real night there in that bedroom with me?"

I was a little worried it was too much for me, as a mere doll, to suggest spending a *real night* together, but he just smiled broadly. "What's for dinner?" he asked.

Still, it was miserable the second day, and the third, playing at being a doll. Listening silently as he spoke was one thing, but it was hard to bear it when he put his hand inside my dress, stroked me all over, and licked the exposed parts of my body. As time went by, though, I got used to it, wanting him to touch me even more. I could hardly wait for the time when I could become a doll, and grew to hate it when night drew to a close.

But last night was different.

I'd felt feverish since morning, my abdomen throbbing in pain, and by noon I couldn't stand. I lay down on the sofa in the living room, pulled up a blanket, and closed my eyes. As soon as I did, though, the ticking of the clock bothered me and I couldn't fall asleep. I shoved the clock underneath the sofa and was finally able to sleep a little, though the pain didn't subside.

Evening came and Takahiro returned. He was worried when he saw my pale face, and when I apologized for not having dinner ready he told me not to worry.

His kind words made me let my guard down, and that was a mistake. "I'd like to sleep here tonight," I told him. "No, I won't allow that," Takahiro said in an icy tone. I don't know why I got so angry, but last night I was really upset, and rage welled up in me.

"Don't make me play along with your perverted games when I'm feeling like this!" I shouted.

Right after I yelled this out, I felt a sharp pain in my cheek.

"What did you just say?"

Takahiro pressed his face close to me, and the way he looked frightened me. But I didn't flinch. I was irritated beyond belief.

"I said you're perverted. Don't tell me you don't realize you're a pervert?"

A loud shout, then another sharp pain in my cheek and I collapsed on the floor. He straddled my still-throbbing abdomen and grabbed my neck with both hands.

"Take it back! If you take it back right this instant, I'll forgive you. Get down on your hands and knees and apologize!"

That's when it happened. I felt something warm and sticky flowing from my crotch. Without getting up and looking I knew what it was, could picture the color. In the next instant, like a speeded-up film, that murder ran through my head.

Kids playing ball, a man showing up in work clothes appraising each child one by one, Emily being led away, the scene inside the changing room...

I'm going to be killed!

I don't remember what happened after that.

Just beyond the dining table where I'm writing this letter, in front of the sofa, Takahiro is lying on the floor. The blood flowing from his head has stopped and is starting to turn dark and thick. Lying next to him is the blood-covered clock. Even from over here it's obvious that he's not breathing.

I must have killed him.

From the images racing through my head from back then, a sudden thought came to me.

We had all addressed the murderer as *ojisan*—uncle—the typical way kids would address an unknown middle-aged man, but actually the man wasn't so old, probably only in his midthirties. And I know now that the person who stole the French dolls was someone else. With the statute of limitations drawing near, I pray with all my heart that these will prove helpful clues, and that the case can be solved now.

Have I fulfilled my promise to you now?

I'm going to mail this letter to you and then fly back to Japan. I have no idea where or how they deal with someone who's killed her husband abroad, but I'm going to go back to Japan and give myself up at the nearest police station.

I might have to go to prison, but that doesn't bother me because I know, once I've served my time, I'll finally live a life that's free. To tell the truth, I feel at peace. As if finally, after all these years, I'm back to a time before you and your family came to town. Back when I breathed that clean, pure air without giving it a second thought.

Take care of yourself.
Goodbye.
Yours,
Sae

An Unscheduled PTA Meeting

Thank you all for coming to this unscheduled meeting of the Wakaba Third Public Elementary School PTA. I know you must all be busy, and I appreciate your coming out despite the rain. I'm Ms. Shinohara.

Normally someone in a higher position—the principal or vice-principal—would be standing here, but the only adult who can explain best what you as parents, and those of you from the community, want to know is me, so I insisted on being allowed to speak to you.

What I'm going to say has not been written down and checked beforehand, so if by chance I happen to say something thoughtless, it's entirely my responsibility, not the school's. Please keep this mind.

I'd like to begin by discussing the events that took place at the beginning of this month at our school, the incident in which a child was injured.

This took place on Wednesday, July fifth, around 11:45 a.m. at the outdoor pool on the school grounds. On that day Classes 1 and 2 of the fourth grade had a combined swimming class. It was sunny, a perfect day for being in the pool. The class took place during the third and fourth periods, starting at 10:40 and scheduled to end at 12:20. I'm homeroom teacher for Class 1, and Mr. Tanabe is homeroom teacher for Class 2, and he and I were in charge.

From the entrance of this gymnasium you're in now, the pool is on the right-hand side, diagonally across the school playground. Seen from the school buildings, from Building Number 3, which is farthest from the main gate, you go out from the place where the children change from outdoor shoes to slippers, pass by the horizontal bars and vertical climbing poles, and at the end you come to the pool. At the entrance to the pool there's a metal sliding gate.

The only entrance is that one, facing the playground.

Except for when the pool is being used for class or for the swim club, the gate is padlocked from the outside, but when the pool is in use we leave it unlocked since we never expect any intruders to come in. We also do that to make it easy for any child who is feeling sick to go straight to the nurse's office, which is on the first floor of Building Number 3.

There's a storage case right inside the entrance where children store their shoes, then it's just a few steps up to the pool. The changing rooms and showers are in the back, so the children proceed past the side of the pool where the springboards are, which is a little wider than the other side, then put on their swimsuits in the changing rooms, take a disinfectant shower, and assemble next to the springboards. In the back, beyond the chain link fence, is a privately owned tangerine orchard.

I hope you can picture the layout from this.

Whenever we have a swimming class, the parents must check off and sign a health form, so they know exactly when their children will be having a swimming class.

In TV interviews, however, several of the parents of children in my class insisted that the school had never informed them that their children were having a swim class that day. I find that hard to fathom.

The schedule for swimming classes is also printed in bold on the monthly class schedule sent out to everyone because some children need a doctor's permission to participate. A separate schedule of swimming classes was also distributed.

Please don't misunderstand me. I'm not trying to be sarcastic. I want everyone to consider all this not from the standpoint of the victim, but from that of adults responsible for protecting the children, and of the parents and people in the community.

As the schedule indicated, fourth graders had swim class scheduled for eight times in the first semester, twice a week starting the third week of June. The day in question was the seventh class. By then the pupils were completely used to swimming and all seventy in the two combined classes were able to swim twenty-five meters, so none of the children were having any particular problems, and class was going smoothly.

During the final thirty minutes of class we time the pupils

to see how long it takes them to swim freestyle for twenty-five meters, so at 11:35, when we were in the fourth period, the pupils were practicing for this, and we went down the alphabetical class list, having them swimming in the lanes.

There are six lanes—lanes one to three, nearest the playground, were for Class 1, and lanes four to six for Class 2. So I was on the playground side, and Mr. Tanabe was by the changing rooms, each of us supervising and instructing the children in our respective classes.

There were approximately twelve children using each lane, divided according to the alphabetical list, with three children in each lane at any one time, with about five meters separating each one of them. The rest of the children were seated in front of the springboard.

It was 11:45 by my watch and I was thinking we should start timing the children. That's when that man, Sekiguchi, broke in.

Kazuya Sekiguchi, thirty-five, unemployed, the TV news said.

I'd like to ask a favor of you. As you listen to what I have to say, please try to imagine the way things were at the time of the incident. Put the photos you've seen on TV out of your mind.

On TV they showed a photo of Sekiguchi from high school, where he looked like a slim, pale, and meek young man, but he was so different in appearance when I saw him you wouldn't know it's the same person. He was a little shorter than me, around five foot five, but he was very heavy, probably over twice my weight, well over two hundred pounds.

Picture that, please.

I'd been a teacher for three years, and Mr. Tanabe for six, so he was in charge of the class. I looked at my watch, saw it was time to start timed swimming, and turned toward Mr. Tanabe and blew the whistle hanging around my neck and raised a hand to signal him.

That's when it happened. A man, wearing some kind of military uniform, leaped out from behind the changing rooms. He was clutching a survival knife, one that was over seven inches long. Not sure what was happening, I blew my whistle as loudly as I could.

Mr. Tanabe, surprised, turned around and noticed Sekiguchi, and the children started screaming. Sekiguchi plowed into Mr. Tanabe, sending him falling into the pool. Then he raised his knife up high and turned toward the children sitting by the poolside. The children screamed but were frozen in fear.

"This country's about to collapse!" Sekiguchi yelled, and charged at the children. "Choose to die a manly death over being taken prisoner!"

I raced toward them. I ran around half the pool but saw nothing I could use as a weapon. All I had on was my swimsuit. Sekiguchi grabbed the child in front of the line for lane six, Ikeda, by the arm and brandished his knife. Still blowing my whistle like mad, I leaped at him. Like I was rolling on the court in volleyball to receive a serve, I leaped at Sekiguchi and grabbed him by the legs. The momentum threw him sideways and he knifed himself in the thigh. He grabbed at the wound with both hands, and tumbled one complete turn and fell into the pool.

Maybe because of the pain, or because he couldn't swim, or because he was so overweight, Sekiguchi shouted "Help!" and started struggling in the water like he was drowning.

The children still in the pool hurriedly scrambled out. I told them to run away to the playground, and I used the phone in the boys' changing room to contact the office and have them call for an ambulance.

Ikeda had been stabbed in the left side.

There were towel racks in the changing room, so I grabbed some towels hanging there and pressed them on Ikeda's wound to stop the bleeding. As I was doing this Ms. Okui, the school nurse, came running up, and she took over. Just then I spotted Sekiguchi, hands on the side of the pool, trying to clamber out.

I ran over to him and took a running kick at his face. After this, other teachers and the ambulance showed up.

That's what happened at the time.

Fortunately—I'm not sure *fortunately* is at all the best way to say it since he was hurt so badly—Ikeda, though still in the hospital with a severe injury that will keep him there for a good month, will recover. There were a couple of children who fell and scraped their knees while running away, but no other children were hurt by Sekiguchi.

Parents and people in town here learned what happened from their children, of course, and then the media got the story out via newspapers, TV, and the Internet, and the whole country soon heard about it.

I did my very best at the time. I feel very sorry for Ikeda, but I think my actions kept his injuries to a minimum. Despite this, the school's been denounced, not just by all of you, but by people living far away, people I've never laid eyes on.

The first target of the attacks was Mr. Tanabe.

After he was shoved into the pool by Sekiguchi, he stayed there, mostly underwater, until the police arrived, even though this elementary school pool is only one meter deep. Ikeda, who was stabbed, was in Mr. Tanabe's class, and when one child's father asked him what Mr. Tanabe was doing while all this was going on, the child responded, "Ms. Shinohara pushed the bad guy and helped us, but Mr. Tanabe was hiding in the pool the whole time." The same sort of conversation took place in many of the children's families, apparently.

The children weren't lying. Mr. Tanabe really *was* hiding. I can't understand it—a male teacher like him, abandoning his kids to hide by himself. Because of his actions Mr. Tanabe became known all over Japan as a weak, cowardly teacher.

You might think Mr. Tanabe, tall, with an athletic build that took him all the way to the nationals in tennis, wouldn't have been afraid enough of that slender man in the photograph to hide. Do you understand now why I started by describing Sekiguchi to you? Do you still think Mr. Tanabe was a weakling and a coward?

What would all of you have done if you'd been in his position?

Human beings have very selfish ways of thinking.

Take the movie *Titanic*. Didn't you project yourself into that scene, imagining yourself on that luxury liner as it went down? Didn't you imagine that you alone were rescued?

Didn't you picture yourself calmly finding a board, climbing onto it, uninjured, and waiting for help?

When you watch TV news scenes of an earthquake or fire, don't you imagine yourself as the only one adroitly dodging the collapsing buildings and running to safety? When you hear news about some random knife attack on the streets, don't you imagine yourself narrowly escaping? When you heard about a suspicious character breaking into school grounds, didn't you picture yourself taking quick-witted action and driving the person away?

Didn't you lash out, asking what this incompetent teacher thought he was doing, because you were so positive that you would have reacted differently? But make no mistake about it—it's precisely people who are convinced they could actually put these self-serving scenarios into practice who, when push comes to shove, aren't able to do a thing.

"Okay, then what about *you?*" people ask. "Do you think you're braver than most because you charged right at Sekiguchi?"...A lot of people must think that. Actually, after the incident, when reports came out talking about me as the *courageous female teacher*, I received countless emails sent to the address we use in the class communications tree telling me to stop being so full of myself.

But the issue goes back further than that. I am not at all what you'd call courageous.

The way I see it, people who are able to take the appropriate actions in an emergency either have had a lot of training to do so, or have experienced something similar in the past.

For me, it's the latter.

*   *   *

This happened fifteen years ago, in the summer when I was in fourth grade.

I went to college in the prefecture we're in now, took the prefectural certification test to be a teacher, and was hired as a teacher here in this small seaside town at the Wakaba Third Public Elementary School. But the town I was born and raised in was completely different.

—— Town. Do any of you know it?

It's a small town in a mountain valley, the size and population about the same as our town here. And economically, too, the two towns are similar, with our town here relying on a factory run by a shipbuilding corporation. Because the towns are so alike, then, when I was assigned to what was seen as an out-of-the-way part of the prefecture, I felt as if I belonged.

When I ask the children to describe their town they say things like "The sea is beautiful," or "There's a lot of natural beauty." Both correct. But aren't they just repeating what they were taught in class in the lower grades? I think you can't really appreciate the town you live in until you've left it.

In the town I grew up in we were taught in elementary school that our town had very clean, pure air.

We were taught that because, at the end of third grade, the Adachi Manufacturing Company built a factory there to manufacture precision instruments. But when I lived there I never really appreciated it.

The air here, too, is wonderful, the smell of the tide when you take a deep breath. But when I was assigned here I bought a small car to commute to school. Early in the second year the rim of the metal parts had already started to rust out. When I saw that, I realized all over again how clean and pure the air was back in my hometown.

And it was in an elementary school back in that little town that a murder took place.

The incident that happened here recently was heavily reported on for the first three days, but after a month it seems like everyone had completely forgotten about it, except those in town. A murder takes place somewhere in Japan nearly every other day, so it's hard to get people to remember one for very long. And there's no need to, unless it directly affects you.

In the same way, the murder that happened in my hometown, since it took place at an elementary school, was widely reported at first, but now I doubt anyone here remembers it.

It happened on August fourteenth.

As I said, the towns are about the same size, so picture your own town fifteen years ago and I think you can understand what I'm saying. Back then, for country children with their grandparents under the same roof, the Obon holiday was nothing special. It was actually kind of a boring day. With relatives visiting from the big cities, we were in the way at home and our parents yelled at us to "go outside and play." But the pool at school was closed, and if we went to the riverside to play our parents would get upset at us, telling us how the spirits of the dead would come out of the water and grab our legs.

There were no recreational facilities in town, not even any mini-mart. In the morning I visited the family grave site with my immediate family and other relatives, had an early lunch, and then, until the sun set, had to wander about this boring town aimlessly, like a refugee.

But there were lots of kids in the same boat. Not just me, but the girls in the West District I always played with, my classmates Sae, Akiko, and Yuka, were at loose ends just like me. Fortunately there was the elementary school in our district and, as we often did, we gathered to play at the school grounds.

There was a girl named Emily with us then. She wasn't born in the town.

From the time we entered elementary school it was always my job to decide what kind of games we would play. Probably because I was so tall, even with my classmates I was always treated like an older student.

For instance, when we were playing by the river once and one of the children's shoes was washed away, it was me they looked to for help. Not that they asked me directly to fetch it. It was more like "Maki, what do we do?" Then of course I had to go retrieve it. I ran downstream, gingerly stepped into the river in my bare feet, lay in wait for the shoe as it floated toward me, and then somehow grabbed it. "We knew you'd get it, Maki!" they cried out, making me feel as if I were their older sister or something.

It wasn't just the kids who treated me like that. Once when we were walking home from school as a group and one of the children fell down and started to cry, an adult passing by scolded me: "You're older so you've got to keep an eye on them." The same thing at school. If one of the other kids was left out, it was always me the teacher came to, to make sure the child was invited to join in.

My parents had always acted that way toward me too. I was the older of two sisters so it was natural to be treated that way at home, but whenever there was an event, like a festival, they always made me take on some major role in any activity where the kids were the focus. The school had a local volunteer corps, and when I didn't participate and my mother found out the other neighborhood kids had, she poked me angrily in the head and back, and after that, unless I had some other important thing going on I always took part.

Because of this, people in town always said I was *mature and reliable*. And after I heard this enough times I started to believe them, to see myself as exactly that. So I thought it only natural that I take control of any situation. If anything, I thought I *had* to. When we were playing, too, I always wracked my brain to figure out what would be most fun.

You might be wondering why I'm bringing this up. But it's connected to the attack at the pool, so I'd appreciate it if you would be patient with me a little longer.

Everything changed in fourth grade, however. With the new plant built by Adachi Manufacturing in our town, we suddenly had lots of transfer students in school. A girl named Emily joined my class. Emily's father was an executive with Adachi and she was really good at school and knew all kinds of things about politics and economics that we country kids had no idea about. She could, for instance, explain what a strong exchange rate for the yen meant, and what effect this would have domestically.

One day our social studies teacher told us that the town we lived in had particularly clean air. None of us were really convinced, but after class someone asked Emily and because she confirmed it, then most of the kids believed it was true.

Because whatever Emily said was correct.

After that, whenever kids in the class were trying to decide something, they always asked Emily's opinion. Even for activities that being from the city didn't help with—like deciding who should be assigned the various chores in the classroom, or what we would do at various events. That had all been my role, but no more.

I had mixed feelings about this, but everything Emily said really was correct, and the ideas she had were always fresh and intriguing and, unable to object, I went along. But I'll admit that being told that the kinds of games my friends and I were involved in were silly wasn't much fun.

Just before Emily moved into town, it was popular among the girls I knew to visit others' houses to see the French dolls on display. Naturally, I was the one who first proposed it. All of us were really into it until the time Emily joined us and said, flatly, that she preferred Barbie dolls. From the next day on, our French doll obsession was over.

Before Emily could take the lead I proposed a new game for us to play—Explorers.

A little outside of town, in a valley, there was an abandoned house. It was a modern-looking Western-style house that apparently hadn't been used for many years. A rich CEO of a company in Tokyo had built it as a summer house for his daughter, who was sickly, but when it was nearly completed his daughter passed away and they left it as is without ever using it. That was the rumor among us kids at the time, and we took it at face value, but the truth was it built as a model house by a resort development company that wanted to sell lots for summer houses in town, but before it was completed the company went bankrupt and the house was left as is. It was only much later, though, that we learned this.

Adults had warned us not to go near the house, and the windows and doors were all boarded up so people couldn't get inside, so up till then we hadn't gone near the place. But one day Yuka, whose family had a grape orchard next door, told us that the board on the back door of the place had come off and that it was easy to pick the lock with a hairpin, so I invited my usual group of friends, plus Emily, to go there.

Playing Explorers was so much fun we forgot all about French dolls. We were the only ones who knew you could get into the house. Inside there were just a few built-in pieces of furniture, but with its faux fireplace and canopied bed it felt like being in a castle. The fun we had there, though—eating sweets and having a party, each of us hiding some treasure of ours inside the fireplace—lasted less than half a month.

One day Emily suddenly told us she didn't want to go there anymore. On top of this she said, "I told Papa about going into the abandoned house." We asked why she'd do something like that, but she wouldn't tell us the reason. I don't know if it was her father who did this, but when we went back later the door had a stronger lock on it so no one could get in.

But I kept on playing with Emily because the next thing she proposed we do was practice volleyball. I'd already decided to join the volleyball club when I got into fifth grade and had pestered my parents over and over to buy me a volleyball, but they kept telling me they wouldn't until I was in the club. Emily, though, owned a ball. Not only that, it was a famous-brand volleyball, the kind used in national tournaments. I think I tried to be friends with her just so I'd get the chance to use the same ball that the Japanese national team used on TV.

On the day of the murder, too, we were playing volleyball.

I'd said to my friends, "Hey, let's go play volleyball at the school playground," and asked Emily to bring her ball from home.

It was sunny that day. You might picture a town in a valley as cool, but the sun was so hot that day it was hard to believe it was getting toward the end of summer. So hot your exposed arms and legs started to sting, even if you were just outside a little while. Emily had said, "It's too hot, so why don't we go to my house and watch Disney videos?" but we'd all been strongly warned not to visit other people's homes during Obon because we'd be in the way during this busy time, so my idea won out.

The other thing was that I didn't really like Emily's house. There were just so many beautiful things there that it made me feel sorry for myself. I think the other kids felt the same way.

Complaining about the heat, we went over next to the gym, in the shade, and began playing. We formed a circle and passed the ball, and we got the idea of trying to pass it a hundred times in a row. Emily was the one who suggested it. "If we're going to play we might as well have a goal," she said. "That way we'll feel happy about accomplishing something." We followed her suggestion, and when we had passed eighty times in a row, all of us were pretty worked up, shouting encouragement to each other.

That's the kind of child Emily was.

We'd just reached ninety times in a row for the first time when a man in work clothes came up to us. He didn't have a survival knife in his hand and didn't yell. He just strolled over to us, came to a halt, and said this, smiling:

"I came to check the ventilation fans in the pool changing rooms, but I forgot to bring a stepladder. I just have to tighten some screws so I was wondering if one of you could get on my shoulders and help out."

That's my role, I thought, and told him I'd help. The other kids all volunteered too, but the man said I was too tall, one of the others was too short, one had glasses, one looked too heavy, and in the end he chose Emily. *Always Emily*, I thought.

I was so disappointed and said, "Let's *all* help out!" Everyone agreed, but the man said, "No, it's too dangerous," and rejected the idea. "If you all wait here I'll buy you ice cream," he said. And he took Emily by the hand and led her off toward the pool.

I wonder how all you parents here today teach your children about staying safe. I hope nobody here expects that that's entirely the job of the school.

"My child holds his chopsticks in a funny way. What are you teaching them there in school?" The other day I had a phone call like this. The child was also a fourth grader. What had his parents been doing up till now? Maybe his family had the same idea, that the school is entirely responsible for training children.

Of course we teach the children how to respond. If a suspicious person tries to talk to them on the way home from school they know they're supposed to yell for help, or push the alarm button on their backpack and run away. We make it clear they should never, ever get into a stranger's car. That they should run into a nearby store or house and seek help. That they should avoid deserted streets. That if something happens, they should report it to an adult right away.

There are a lot of parents who take this seriously. There's an online crime prevention service now that sends out alerts whenever there's a report of a suspicious person lurking about, and I think many people must be registered for that service.

Just the other day in my class, one of the girls told me that on the way to school that day at the crosswalk a "weird old guy" had been staring at her. I ran out to check and discovered it was one of the male homeroom teachers for another grade whose turn it was to supervise the school crosswalk. If back in my day we had been as cautious as this girl was, maybe we would have been able to avoid that awful incident.

But there weren't any adults then who reminded children, including us, to be so cautious. To say nothing of the fact that this took place at a school, and the man had on work clothes, and had what seemed like a plausible reason for being there.

After Emily left we went on passing the ball, finally reaching our goal of a hundred times, and then we sat down on the steps of the gym to chat. But still Emily hadn't returned. Before long it started getting dark and the signal for six o'clock started playing. In this town it's the melody "Seven Children," but in the town I grew up in it was "Greensleeves."

We were getting a little concerned about Emily so we went over to the pool to check on her. The location of the school pool there was very similar to the one here. The gate was unlocked the whole summer, so we went right in, walked around the pool, and headed toward the changing rooms. The only sound was that of some cicadas far away.

The changing rooms were unlocked, too. I was in the lead and opened the door to the girls' changing room but neither Emily nor the man was inside. I was a little upset, thinking maybe she'd gone home without saying anything to us, so we went over to the boys' changing room, just to double-check. Akiko was the one who opened it. She slid it open, looking away from the door, and at that instant a horrendous scene leaped out at us.

Emily lay on the floor. Her head was toward the door so we could clearly see her face—the eyes wide open, liquid dripping from her mouth and nose. We called her name over and over but there was no response.

She's dead, I thought. *Something awful's happened*. I think it was a conditioned reflex, but I quickly instructed the other girls what to do.

I told Akiko and Yuka, both fast runners, to go to, respectively, Emily's house and the local police station. Sae, who was the quietest among us, I had stay with the body. And I told them I'd try to find a teacher and tell them what had happened. None of them had any objections, so, leaving Sae behind to keep watch, the three of us dashed off.

Don't you think we were brave? We were only ten years old and had just discovered our friend's dead body, but each of us played our part without any crying or screaming.

At least the other three girls really were brave.

It was closer for the two who were going to Emily's house and the police station to leave by the rear entrance to the school, so once out of the pool area they cut across the playground and ran toward the gate behind the gym. I headed for the school building alone. There were two school buildings side by side. The one facing the playground was Building Number 2, the one facing the main entrance was Number 1. The teachers' office was on the first floor in Number 1.

People often mistakenly think that teachers have summer break off, but that's not true. While the children are on summer vacation the teachers all come to work as usual, from 8 a.m. to 5 p.m. Like in regular companies, they have some paid leave during that time, and get time off for the Obon holiday.

So even during summer vacation there should be some teachers in the teachers' office, at least on a weekday. But as I said, the murder took place on August fourteenth, the middle day of the three-day Obon holiday. The teachers were all on holiday. If it had been morning, there might have been at least one teacher in the school who'd stopped by to take care of something. But it was already past 6 p.m.

I ran over to Building Number 1, but all five doors, including the main entrance into the building, were locked. So I went over to the courtyard between the two buildings to the windows of the teachers' office. Even without standing on tiptoes

I could see into the office through a gap in the shut white curtains, but didn't see anyone inside.

Terror suddenly grabbed me. The man who killed Emily and I might be all alone in the school.... Was he hiding nearby, waiting to grab me and make me his next victim?...Before I knew it, I was running full speed. I ran out of the courtyard, out the main gate, and flew back home without stopping once. Even when I arrived back home I barely slowed down, kicked aside my shoes, ran to my room, slammed the door, and drew the curtains. I scrambled into bed, pulled the covers up, and lay there trembling. *I'm scared—scared, scared.* That's all I could think about.

After a while my mother ran into my room. "Oh, there you are!" she said, and pulled the covers off me. "What in the world happened?" she asked. My mother had been out shopping when I came home and had heard that something terrible had happened at the elementary school and had run right over. In the midst of the uproar there, she looked for me, but not finding me, went home, thinking she needed to tell my father. When she saw my shoes tossed aside at the entrance she hurried to my room.

Through tears I told her what had happened. That Emily was dead inside the changing room at the pool. "Why didn't you tell anyone, and hide under the covers like that?" she said accusingly. "Because I was terrified," I was about to say, when I suddenly wondered about the other children.

I was supposed to be the steady, reliable one, and if I had fled in fright the others must have too. But my mother told me she'd heard from Akiko's mother.

Akiko, accompanied by her older brother, her head bleeding, had come home and reported to her mother, "Something terrible happened to Emily at the pool," and as her mother was about to go check it out, she ran across my mother and they went together to the school. Along the way they passed Sae, being carried on her mother's back as they headed home.

According to my mother, when they got to the pool they found Emily's mother and the local patrolman, along with Yuka, who, though always a bit of a wallflower, clearly related what had taken place.

"What were you doing?" my mother asked me. "You're the one everyone counts on, especially at a time like this. What do you think you were doing, hiding here? It's shameful!

"It's shameful, shameful...." As she repeated this, she smacked me over and over on my head and back. "I'm so sorry," I repeated, blubbering, though I didn't really understand who I was apologizing to, or for what.

I think you get the picture. I was the only one who ran away, while the other three girls did exactly what they were supposed to do. It must have been very frightening to tell Emily's mother she was dead. And to explain everything to the patrolman, a taciturn man with a frightening expression. But staying with the dead body—that must have been the most terrifying of all.

I knew now I was a complete coward. Not only that, but the murder had taken something else—something very important—away from me.

My very reason to exist.

The police questioned me alone about Emily's murder, but

more often the four of us were questioned together, or with our parents and teachers along. Which direction did the man come from? What did he say when he first spoke to you? What about his clothes, his build, his facial features? Did he remind you of anybody, any famous entertainers?

I tried my hardest to remember the day of the murder and set the example in responding to their questions, to make up for the feeling of guilt I had for being the only one who ran away. My mother, who'd come with me, kept poking me surreptitiously in the back, urging me to "Speak up for the other girls."

But I was shocked by what I heard. When the other girls answered the questions they all contradicted what I'd said.

"The man had on gray work clothes."

"No, they weren't gray so much as kind of greenish."

"I think he had sort of narrow eyes."

"Hmm, I didn't feel they were so narrow."

"He had a kind expression."

"No way. He looked that way to you just because he promised to buy us ice cream."

That's how it went. Even after Emily became the leader of our group, the other three had never contradicted any of my opinions. But now they glared at me with this *What are you talking about?* look on their faces and denied everything I said. What's more, though they contradicted what I said, all three of them insisted they *couldn't remember the man's face*. They couldn't remember his face, yet were positive my memories were all wrong.

They must have all known I was the only one who'd run

away. None of them directly criticized me for it, but I know that in their hearts they were angry, and despised me.

You're always acting so big, they were thinking, *but you turn out to be the biggest coward of all. So don't show off.*

If that was all, I shouldn't have had such a guilty conscience, though I did feel ashamed. I mean, I *had* tried to go to the teachers' office. My greatest sin in this whole affair wasn't that I had run away.

I had committed an even greater sin. And today is the first time I've ever confessed it.

I remembered the criminal's face but said I didn't.

When I saw how the other three girls—though they claimed to remember clearly everything from the time the man called out to us to the time we discovered the body—shook their heads and said they couldn't recall the most important thing of all, the man's face, I was stunned. How could you remember everything *except* the man's face? I couldn't accept that. It made me angry, them contradicting my opinions, since I was telling the truth. And I was thinking of telling them that. Of the four, I thought I was the best student, and in my mind I mocked them as a bunch of witless idiots.

But to think I was a bigger coward than any of them...When I thought of this, a certain idea came to me. Each of the other three had carried out her assigned task alone. That must have been far more frightening than when the four of us found the body. And maybe that terror had obliterated any memory of the man's face from their minds.

I remember his face because, after we found the body, I'm the one who *didn't do a thing.*

We were asked what each of us did after we discovered the body, and I responded that since there was no one in the teachers' office I decided to go home to tell an adult what had happened. There were a lot of houses between the school and my house. One was even one of the houses where they'd shown us their French doll. But I passed those places by, went straight home, and even though my father and other relatives were there, didn't say a word to anyone.

If I had told someone, they might have been able to gather more eyewitness information about the man. Only recently did this thought occur to me.

I concluded then that it would be worse to say I remembered the man's face. If I was the only one who answered accurately, the police and my teachers would realize I was the one who didn't do anything, and attack me for it.

Still, I didn't regret saying I couldn't recall his face. In fact, soon afterward I was glad that I had.

That's because they didn't catch the murderer. If, say, I alone said I remembered what he looked like, and the murderer learned of this, I was sure I'd be the next one he killed. By saying I didn't remember, I was protected.

Perhaps this was the period in our lives when we went from being friends with other children just because they were the same age and lived nearby, to finding friends on our own who shared similar interests and ideas. Or maybe it was just because we didn't want to be reminded of the murder. But afterward the four of didn't play together much.

When I went into fifth grade I joined the volleyball club, and in sixth grade ran for vice-president of the student council and was elected. Since a boy always was the president, my mother urged me to run for vice-president. I made new friends, found new areas to be active in, and worked hard to clear my name. In junior high, too, I took the lead in being in student government, and was very active in local volunteer activities.

Even more than before, people said I was a *steady, reliable* girl.

I didn't recognize my behavior as an escape response, and watching the other three girls from afar—Sae, always trembling in fear; Akiko, who kept refusing to go to school; and Yuka, who became a delinquent, going out at night and shoplifting—I was convinced that of all of us I was the one who'd recovered best after the murder. I'd convinced myself I'd done everything I could have after the murder.

That is, until that day.

Three years after Emily's murder, her parents moved back to Tokyo. Her mother said she wouldn't leave town until the murder was solved, but her husband was reassigned to Tokyo and she didn't have a choice. Emily's mother had been so devastated by her daughter's death that she fell ill for a time, and she was, of course, the one who most hoped that the case would be solved. But staying behind and searching for the murderer all by herself was beyond her.

It was in the summer of our first year in junior high when Emily's mother—tall and slender and as beautiful as an actress—called us all to her home. Before she moved away she wanted, one more time, to ask us about what had happened on that terrible day. "This will be the last time," she said. We couldn't refuse.

Her husband's driver came to each of our houses in turn in a huge car to pick us up, and we set off for Emily's home in the Adachi company apartment building, a place the four of us had only visited together once, that one time before. This was the first time since the murder that the four of us had done anything together, but in the car we never spoke of the murder at all. What clubs are you in? we asked each other. How did your final exams go? Harmless topics.

Emily's mother was alone in her home.

It was a sunny Saturday afternoon. The room we were in was like a luxury hotel in Tokyo, with a view of the entire town, and she served us tea, and cakes ordered from Tokyo that had all kinds of fruits on them I'd never heard of before. If only Emily had been there it would have been a very elegant little farewell party. But Emily had been murdered, and a heavy, oppressive feeling that didn't match the sunny weather hung over our gathering.

After we finished the cakes Emily's mother asked us to tell her about the murder. I did most of the talking, but after all four of us had briefly spoken about that day, Emily's mother suddenly burst out in a loud, hysterical voice.

"*Enough* already! You keep repeating the same stupid thing over and over: *I can't remember his face, I can't remember his face.* Because you're such idiots, three years have passed and they haven't arrested the murderer. Emily was killed because she played with idiots like you. It's *your* fault. You're all *murderers!*"

Murderers—in an instant the world changed. We'd suffered in the years since the murder, but not only hadn't we been rewarded for getting through all that, now we were being told that it was *our* fault that Emily had been killed.

Her mother went on. "I will never forgive you, unless you find the murderer before the statute of limitations is up. If you can't do that, then atone for what you've done, in a way I'll accept. If you don't do either one, I'm telling you here and now—I *will* have revenge on each and every one of you. I have far more money and power than your parents, and I'll make you suffer far worse than Emily ever did. I'm her parent, and I'm the only one who has that right."

Emily's mother was, at that moment, far more frightening than the man who had murdered her.

I'm so sorry, but I do remember the man's face.

If only I had said that then, I might not be standing here before you today. But sadly, by that point I really had forgotten the man's face. It wasn't a very memorable face to begin with, and I had told myself over and over that I didn't remember it. Three years was more than enough time for his features to vanish from my mind.

The next day, Emily's mother left town, leaving behind that terrible promise she had made to the four of us children. I don't know what the other girls thought, but I was desperate to think of a way to avoid her retribution.

Catching the criminal seemed impossible. So I chose the latter, performing an act of penance that would satisfy Emily's mother.

* * *

I hope you can understand now why I was able to leap at an intruder brandishing a knife, despite being such a coward. It's only because of these experiences I had in the past.

Mr. Tanabe never had those experiences. That's the only thing that separates us. I was treated as a hero, while he was condemned.

So, was Mr. Tanabe to blame for the incident?

The intruder got inside by climbing over the fence separating the pool and the tangerine orchard. People talk over and over about crime prevention measures, but where is there a school surrounded by high fences like a prison? Is this country rich enough to set up surveillance cameras that cover every inch of every public school? Or to put it another way, before the attack, was anybody here conscious that security had gotten bad enough to require those kind of measures?

I don't think anyone on our citizens' watch patrols who's ever skipped their turn, pretending to be sick, has the right to criticize Mr. Tanabe. Yet all the frustrations that had built up over time led people to lash out at him. I've answered complaining phone calls at school, and since I live in the same dorm for single teachers, I've seen the slanderous notes pasted to his door. The language on some of them is so awful you can hardly stand to look, and it makes me wonder whether whoever wrote them would ever let their children read them. Mr. Tanabe's phone and cell phone ring late at night, and I've even heard what sounds like him throwing the phone against the wall. Someone smashed the windshield of his car, too, in the parking lot.

For these reasons, as I'm sure you're aware, Mr. Tanabe is not in a condition, emotionally, to stand before all of you today.

What in the world did Mr. Tanabe do wrong? If you're angry because your children were put in a terrifying situation, why don't you denounce the man who actually attacked them? Do you refrain from doing that because he was an out-of-work thirty-five-year-old who had been seen at a psychiatric hospital? Or is it because he's the son of a Diet member, the most powerful person in this district?

Or—was it just easier to blame Mr. Tanabe?

I was just his work colleague, but even I felt sympathy for him. Can you imagine how his girlfriend, a girlfriend he's promised to marry, must have felt?

As you're all aware, Mr. Tanabe is tall and good-looking, quite athletic, graduated from a national university, and was very popular with his pupils as well as their parents. When I would visit some of my pupils' homes, some of the mothers even made their preference abundantly clear, telling me they wished it had been Mr. Tanabe who'd stopped by. You can imagine how popular he was among the women teachers. At a conference with other schools once, one of the teachers there even asked me if Mr. Tanabe was seeing anyone.

I can imagine people wanting to ask me, "Don't you like him too?" Actually, I found him a little hard to get along with. When I was first hired at the school Mr. Tanabe came up and said, "Whenever you have anything you want to ask about, feel free to ask me." This was the first time in my life anybody had ever said something like that, and I was overjoyed. But I really don't know how to depend on other people. I know I should have relied on him for help for anything I couldn't do, but the fact is there wasn't anything I couldn't do.

As I got to know him better as a colleague, I started to think I actually disliked him. Mr. Tanabe was a lot like me. And I hated myself.

Being good at academics and sports is not, necessarily, a clear gauge of the caliber of a person. A person's physical size has nothing to do with it. But if you're physically big and can handle things fairly well, people do start to see you as capable and reliable.

Mr. Tanabe must have been told since he was a child, too, that he was very *capable*. Being a boy, maybe he heard this even more than I did.

I think he became overly conscious of this—that he was a capable person. When a problem occurred in his class, instead of consulting with other teachers in the same grade, he struggled to solve it on his own. And he'd even poke his nose into other classes' problems, trying to give them advice.

I have similar tendencies. So I imagine Mr. Tanabe found it hard to get along with me, too.

The woman Mr. Tanabe went out with was a short, slender, fragile, doll-like woman. She was so good with computers she once joked that she'd infected the police with a virus, yet when Mr. Tanabe was passing by once she asked him to show her how to use the printer. All he did was print up a few pages for her, but on her next day off she showed up at his dorm room with some homemade sweets she'd made to thank him for his help. When I saw Mr. Tanabe happily inviting her in, it was the first time I ever realized that relying on others wasn't so hard after all.

I wasn't jealous of her, but she reminded me of one of my friends who'd been with me the day of the murder, and I knew she was the type that I wasn't all that fond of. This woman was Ms. Okui, the school nurse.

Right after Sekiguchi fell into the pool I used the extension phone to call the teachers' office. I told them, "An intruder snuck into the pool area and someone's gotten hurt. Call an ambulance." When I did, the first one to rush to the pool wasn't some sturdy male teacher but the doll-like Ms. Okui. She must have reacted more to the news that someone was injured, rather than to the idea that an intruder was there. Maybe all the male teachers were too busy finding something to use as a weapon.

The day after Mr. Tanabe took an overdose of sleeping pills and was rushed to the hospital, Ms. Okui phoned a publisher and told them she thought I overreacted. Later the same day the following article was posted on a weekly magazine's online site. Don't claim you never saw it.

This female teacher is seen as a hero for boldly leaping at the intruder to protect her pupils, but did she really need to go so far as to take a man's life? The children had all run to safety, yet each time the man, wounded badly in the thigh, raised his face out of the water she kicked it like it was a soccer ball, sending him sinking to the bottom of the pool, until he no longer raised his face anymore. The male teacher at the scene, so in pain from the blows he'd received he couldn't get out of the pool, came face-to-face with a living hell as the pool became a sea of blood. Who, indeed, was the one who snatched away from this male teacher the will to ever return to teaching?

I was supposed to be a hero, but after that article came out I was suddenly viewed as a murderer.

Pretty amazing to see how the power of love can move public opinion.

I'm thinking you all must have been happy about that, for now you had a new object of scorn. You were the ones who had driven Mr. Tanabe to the wall, but now you felt sorry for him, making it seem like I was the one who'd done that. And you blamed me now for all the incompetence your children had displayed before the incident, claiming it was my fault they hardly talked and were having trouble concentrating. I think it was an escape valve for you all, a way to relieve your own day-to-day stress. When someone demanded that I pay them to replace the blood-soaked towel, I couldn't believe my ears.

Fire the murderer teacher! Get down on your hands and knees and apologize! Take responsibility for what you did!

Which explains why we're holding this unscheduled PTA meeting today, and why I'm standing here before you. But I wonder if the reason I have to be attacked like this is because none of the children died.

Do you think I pointlessly kicked to death a poor, feeble, ill young man?

Would it have been better for me to wait until he'd killed

four or five people? Should I have followed the lead of my cowardly colleague, pretended to be pushed into the pool, and hid there silently as he attacked the children?

Or would it have satisfied you if I had died along with the man?

I wish I had never saved your children.

Right after the attack started, the man stabbed himself and fell into the pool, so there's an issue here that precedes any talk of legitimate self-defense. But as luck would have it, the man's father is an influential person in this area, so it would appear an arrest warrant for me is about to be issued.

Perhaps a kindly detective is among you, giving me a chance to finish speaking first. If that's the case, there's one more thing I'd like to say.

On the weekly magazine website it said *each time* the man lifted his face from the water, but to be precise, I kicked him only once. So if it comes to trial the question will be whether or not, in that one kick, I had murderous intent. When I think that the jurors might come from among you all, it makes me shudder.

I am not going to reveal any more facts to you all. That would be pointless. What I'm about to say now is directed at only one particular person among you.

I would like to thank you again for coming from so far away to be here today.

Asako.

To me, the penance you laid on us meant I should grow up to be a good person, the kind Emily would be proud of. I knew

I wasn't really reliable, wasn't capable, yet as penance I served in student government in junior high, became class president in high school, was captain of the volleyball team too, studied hard, and went to college.

I went to a college in this part of the country because I wanted to live near the ocean. I felt that a town next to the ocean, where you could see the Pacific Ocean, would have a much more open, free feeling to it than the cramped little valley town I'd called home. I was quite mistaken about that, but I never thought of returning to my hometown.

After graduating from college, I got a position as an elementary school teacher.

To tell the truth, I'm not all that fond of children. But if I liked my job that wouldn't constitute penance. I felt that I had to put myself in the kind of place where I had failed, and do my very best there.

It's only been a little over two years since I started the job, but I've always come to work before anyone else, have always made it a point to listen to all the silly things the children had to say, have always responded properly to the useless complaints the parents might have, and I have always made sure to take care of any office-type work I needed to do that day, even if it meant staying late.

And I'd had enough, quite enough of it. I couldn't stand it anymore and felt like crying. I could barely keep myself from running away. I wasn't without friends I could commiserate with. I did talk to and email some people from my college volleyball team, spilling my complaints about work to them. But all they did was share similar gripes.

"That's not like you, Maki, to complain like that. Hang in there!"

But what does that mean, anyway, to be *like me*? Does it mean I seem to have it together, when in fact I don't? The only people who know the real me are the three girls at the time of the murder. They and no one else. When I realized that, I started to miss them terribly.

I have nothing to do with the three of them directly anymore, but my younger sister, who went to a nearby vocational school and remained in our hometown, does give me reports of what the other girls are doing.

Sae got married and was going to live abroad, I heard. Her fiancé was some elite man, apparently. Akiko is, as before, pretty much a shut-in, but according to my sister she saw her taking her older brother's child out shopping and she seemed to be enjoying herself. Yuka is back home now, expecting a baby soon.

This is what I heard about them at the beginning of last month. It made me suddenly feel stupid, suffering as I am to do my penance. Everyone else seems to have completely forgotten the murder, and the promise they made to you.

If you think about it calmly, though, it seems unlikely that you would actually take revenge on us if we didn't keep our promise. You must have told us that in order to boost our level of resolve.

I'm the only one who remained obsessed about the murder. The only one who stupidly took you at your word and lived out my penance. At least it seemed that way to me.

It struck me as silly to keep working as hard as I had been, and I started to slack off at work. When some parents don't pay the school lunch fee, we're supposed to pay them a visit, but now I just ignored it. I mean, it wasn't going to come out of my salary, was it? When I got calls in the morning about children staying home because they weren't feeling well, I didn't pursue the matter and see whether it was a real illness or if they were faking it. I just marked them down as absent. When the kids got into some silly argument and called each other names, I'd just let them keep at it until they settled down. That's how I started to think.

Once I adopted that stance, things got so much easier. And the children seemed to like me better. Perhaps being so hard on myself had made them, too, uncomfortable, and stifled people around me.

Just around that time the name of one of the girls—Sae—was on the news on TV. They said that soon after she married she'd killed her husband, who was some kind of sexual pervert. Not long after this I got a letter from you, which was sent to my parents' place. You didn't include a message, just a copy of a letter Sae had written to you.

For the first time I learned how Sae had felt these past fifteen years. My thoughtless order to her to guard Emily's dead body had produced a life of fear I could never have imagined. If only I had gone back to the pool after finding the teachers' office deserted...

In her own way, Sae had kept her promise to do penance. She loved those French dolls so much, and of the four of us was herself most like one of them, so quiet, so mild-mannered. But still, she was much braver than I ever was.

Even after fifteen years I was still the biggest coward of all.

And then that intruder broke into our school. As I said, it was a beautiful, sunny summer day at the school pool. And the ones who were about to be assaulted right before my eyes were fourth graders. So many of the conditions were the same as fifteen years ago that it made me think that maybe you had planned it all, that you were lying in wait, watching it unfold.

Running away meant that I'd never be able to escape that murder, even after the statute of limitations ran out. This time I didn't hesitate. It would be better to end up stabbed, I decided, than living the rest of my life as a coward.

By the time these thoughts came, I was already dashing toward Sekiguchi.

I knew in an instant now why I had become an elementary school teacher. The intense training I endured on the volleyball team—it had all led up to this day. Now was my only chance to regain what I had lost. That's what I was thinking as I leaped at Sekiguchi's legs.

It never entered my mind to strike Sekiguchi down or to kill him. All I was thinking was: *I can't let the children with me get killed. I have to protect them at all costs. This time I have to do what needs to be done.*

There's one point about Ms. Okui's testimony that I need to correct. She said *the children had all run to safety,* but when the man was trying to climb out of the pool there was still one child beside the pool. Ikeda, the boy who'd been stabbed. And with him was Ms. Okui. I didn't think she was capable of protecting Ikeda. Nor did I want her to. There was only one who could handle it. Me.

I think I finally understand Mr. Tanabe's feelings. Perhaps it really *was* my fault that he took those sleeping pills.

Ikeda was screaming out, "It hurts! It hurts!" The towel pressed against his wound had turned red. A sudden thought hit me: Hadn't Emily, too, when she was attacked by that man, yelled out? Ever since the murder I'd been obsessed by my own cowardice, and had imagined the fear the other three girls must have had, in order to measure it against my own fear.

But I'd never thought about Emily. And how she must have felt.

She must have felt the greatest terror of all. She must have cried out for help, over and over. And yet we never went to see how she was doing. Emily—I am so very sorry. This was the first time I thought this.

At the same moment, I was not about to let some pervert, an adult, attack weak, defenseless children. Our lives had been ruined by an idiot adult, and there was no way I was going to let it happen again.

The man had already swung his uninjured leg up onto the poolside deck. The thought that such an adult existed had me so upset I dashed straight toward him.

Sekiguchi's expressionless, wet face overlapped in my mind with that of the man from fifteen years ago. I kicked that face as hard as I could, and in that instant I felt my penance was complete. That I'd kept my promise.

But that wasn't what I really had to do to keep my promise.

A coward's penance is completed only by stepping up and con-fessing.

The instant I kicked Sekiguchi's face, the face of the man from fifteen years ago rose up clearly in my mind.

Over the last few years I've had a sense that Emily's mur-derer, with his almond eyes and lucid face, was good-looking. Back when the police asked me whether the man reminded me of any celebrities, I couldn't think of a single one. Now, though, I could list a few. That costar on the Thursday-night TV drama, or that Prince Somebody who's a jazz pianist, or that *kyogen* actor...All of them young men.

As Sae said in her letter, the man wasn't all that old at the time—not the type we'd call "uncle."

But when I consider what that face must look like fifteen years on, I'm not reminded of any celebrities as much as of Hiroaki Nanjo, the man who operates that free school for dropouts. The one in the news when there was an arson inci-dent at his school last summer. Don't get me wrong—I'm not accusing Mr. Nanjo of being the murderer.

There's someone else the murderer resembles even more. But saying the name out loud is insensitive, I think. That per-son isn't alive anymore, so I won't.

I am hoping with all my heart that this may be a clue that will help catch the murderer.

But is that what you really want?

I truly feel awful that you lost your precious daughter, your only child. I know that fifteen years ago, and even today, you're the one who's praying most that the murderer is finally caught. But wasn't it a mistake to make those girls who were playing with your daughter take on all the sorrow you felt at losing her? And take on your anxiety, your feelings of impotence, that the murderer was still at large?

Sae and I remained in the clutches of that murder all these years not because of the murderer, but because of *you*, Asako-san. Wouldn't you agree? Isn't that why you've come all the way here to witness the penance of one of those children from years ago?

There are two more of us. My hope is that the mistaken acts of penance stop here. Though there's nothing I can do about that.

Nothing I can do.... I like the sound of that.

That's all I'll say here. Do not take it the wrong way, but I won't be answering any questions....

The Bear Siblings

I really loved my older brother.

He's the one who taught me how to do flips on the horizontal bar, how to jump rope, and how to ride a bike. I'm pretty coordinated, but it takes me time to grasp things, yet my brother never got upset. He was always patient, coaching me until I got it right, until it got dark.

"Hang in there! Just a little more! I know you can do it, Akiko!" That's how he encouraged me.

Even now when I gaze at the sunset I can hear my brother's voice encouraging me. And on that day it was my brother, too, who came to get me.

That day? I mean the day Emily was murdered.

You're a professional counselor, right? You told me you wanted to hear about the murder, so that's what I'll tell you about. Where should I start? The other three girls are much more reliable than me, and smarter, so it'd be a lot easier if you asked them about when we were all together. You still want to hear my story?

Okay, then I'll just talk about later, when I was alone with Emily.

Still, it's kind of odd that now, after all this time, you'd want to hear about this....

Oh, I get it. It's because the statute of limitations on the murder will run out soon.

On that day I was in a wonderful mood from the morning. The day before, my aunt Yoko came home for the Obon holiday and brought me a new piece of clothing as a present. I had it on, which is why I felt so happy.

My aunt worked at a department store in one of the cities in the prefecture, and always bought me and my brother clothes as presents when she came back to town. Up till then it had always been matching sports shirts for me and my brother, or other boyish kinds of clothes. But that year was different. "Akiko, you're in fourth grade now," she told me, "so how about wearing something a little more girly?" She'd bought me an adorable pink blouse with ribbons and frills.

It was a fluffy, glittery design, like something a rich little girl would wear. "Is it really okay for me to wear this?" I asked, hardly believing it as I held it up, spellbound, against my chest. My parents and relatives around me all burst out laughing.

"Are you sure you should give this to Akiko?" my father asked. He could speak so bluntly like that because it was his own older sister who'd bought the blouse—ten times more expensive than anything I'd had before—but I'm sure everyone was thinking the same thing. "It looks cute," my older brother piped up, but even Aunt Yoko, who'd bought it for me, smiled wryly as if having some doubts herself.

Though not as sturdily built as I am now, of course, back in elementary school I was nevertheless big-boned and solid. My clothes were all hand-me-downs from my brother, who was two years older. Some of the boys in my class made fun of me, calling me a Boy-Girl. But I was used to it. It was always that way.

Still, it could have been worse—at least they treated me like a human being. But my parents and relatives always said the two of us were like a couple of bear siblings. Actually, on Valentine's Day and his birthday my brother often got Winnie-the-Pooh trinkets from girls, who said he reminded them of the storybook bear. My brother wasn't one of the more popular kids, but the girls did seem to like him despite his looks.

Boys have it easy. Even if they look like a bear they're popular, provided they can play sports. And being big isn't a drawback the way it is for girls.

"If only you had been born a boy, Akiko," my mother often told me. She didn't mean I'd be more popular or anything. She just regretted having to spend extra money on a girls' gym outfit and swimsuit for me to use at school.

Come to think of it, I was talking about this very thing to Emily that day.

*　　*　　*

I'd gone with my relatives to the local temple, and after we ate lunch I found some other kids with time on their hands hanging around outside, and before I knew it the usual little group of girls had assembled. My classmates from the West District—Sae, Maki, and Yuka. We were hanging around in front of the little cigarette shop, just chatting, when Emily came walking down the slope toward us. She said she'd seen us from the window of her apartment. Her house was the highest point in the whole town.

Maki suggested we go play volleyball at the school playground, so Emily went back to her house to get her volleyball and I went with her.

"Akiko? Why don't you go with Emily?" Maki said. "'Cause you're a fast runner." Not that this means I ran all the way. Bringing up running was just an excuse so that Maki could get her way. I knew this, but getting her angry would only lead to trouble, and since I always depended on her, I did what she said without a word. I think the other two girls felt the same.

So I walked together with Emily up the gentle slope back to her towering, castlelike apartment building. We'd often played since she transferred to our school in April, but this was the first time we'd ever been alone together. I wasn't the talkative type and didn't know what I should talk about, so I walked along in silence.

"That blouse is really cute," Emily suddenly said. "It's from Pink House, right? I love their clothes."

She was talking about my new blouse. My family had mercilessly made fun of me about wearing it, but when I wore it to the temple it seemed to, surprisingly, look good on me.

My father teased me, saying, "Akiko, you look like a girl!" My mother, impressed, commented, "Someone who works in a department store really does know how to select nice things!" So I was in a great mood.

"That blouse is your Sunday best, so change into something else and go out and play," my mother said after we got home from the temple, but I wanted to show off the blouse to everyone so I kept it on.

The girls I always played with, though, didn't say a thing about it. My brother often explained to me what he called the "ironclad rules" of country folk. Among them was the rule that you could envy things you could actually get, but should ignore things that were out of reach. Without realizing it, the other girls maybe had been putting that rule into practice. Or maybe they weren't interested at all in what I was wearing. Not that I brought up the new blouse myself, because I didn't.

But Emily noticed my blouse. *Fashionable Tokyo children like her really are different,* I thought. The problem was, though she'd praised my blouse, I had no idea about the brand she'd mentioned, Pink House. It was embarrassing, but I wanted to know more about it, so I asked her. She told me Pink House made lots of soft, puffy clothes with frills and ribbons and corsages and badges, like something out of *Anne of Green Gables* or *Little Women*. "It's a brand," she explained, "that fulfills the dreams of girls who love cute things."

I imagined a shop filled with cute clothes like that. *I'd love to go there,* I thought. How wonderful it would be to have a chest filled with Pink House clothes! Just imagining it had me all excited. Actually, I loved that kind of really girly thing, though I'd always kept that secret.

I mean, nobody expects a bear to be all girly.

French dolls were popular among the girls for a time, and all of us sketched out designs for dresses for them. A gold tiara with a row of hearts, dresses like a field of flowers with pink and white roses scattered about, glass slippers... "Wow!" my friends said in surprise. "Akiko, you can really come up with some cute dresses too!" A pretty rude thing to say if you think about it.

But that's how far I was from being *cute*. Cute things don't suit a bear. So I enjoyed them in secret. That was more than enough for me.

So having Emily praise my clothes made me overjoyed. But she went on and said this: "You're lucky, Akiko, that those cute clothes suit you. My mother says I don't look good in them and won't buy them for me."

It didn't sound like she was making fun of me.

Cute clothes look good on me but not on Emily? No way! A puffy cute design looked good on her, but with her slim build and long legs, it was true that a sharper, more cool type of clothing looked even better. This day Emily was wearing a tight black T-shirt with a pink Barbie logo on it, and a red pleated skirt, and they definitely suited her.

And yet here she was, a girl like Emily, saying over and over again how she envied me my new blouse. It made me happy in the beginning, but then I got a little embarrassed and made some silly excuse.

"My aunt works in a department store and bought this with

an employee's discount. My mother would never buy something this expensive. I always wear my brother's hand-me-downs. I don't complain, but she tells me it would have been better if I'd been a boy."

"My mother says the same thing. *If only you had been a boy.*"

"What? You're kidding! Nobody would say that about *you.*"

"It's true. And not just once. She's said it many times, sounding really disappointed. I hate it."

Emily pouted as she said this, but I just couldn't believe it. With her cool-looking almond eyes, it's true she would have made a good-looking boy, but as a girl she was more than pretty.

Still, it made me so happy to know that Emily had been told the same thing, and made me feel closer to her. I felt as if I could share my love of cute things, and wanted to be even better friends with her.

Even now I regret that it never happened.

As we continued to grumble about our mothers, we arrived at her building. We went through the entrance, past the property manager, and took the elevator to the seventh floor to Emily's apartment, which was on the east side, at the very end. "It's only a four-LDK apartment," she told me, "so it's kind of small," but I had no idea of what LDK—a sort of great room, living room/dining room/kitchen—meant.

Emily pushed the call button and her mother came out. She was so beautiful—slim and tall, with gorgeous big eyes like some actress—that I feel almost bad about calling her a *mother,* putting her in the same category as my own short, stocky mother. I went inside the front door, feeling the cool air of the AC, and waited with Emily's mother as Emily went to her room to retrieve the volleyball.

"Thank you for being friends with Emily. I think it's too hot to play volleyball. You girls should play here, inside. I just got some delicious cake delivered. Invite the other girls over afterward."

Though her voice was refined and kind, I sort of shrank into myself and could only manage a faint smile in response. I might have even forgotten to breathe. Everything in Emily's house was so obviously expensive that all I could think of was trying not to make a wrong move and break anything.

The first time I ever experienced feeling ill at ease was the first evening I was invited to Emily's house.

Just standing in the entryway, I couldn't relax. On top of the shoe case was a vase, the kind that makes you think of the Palace of Versailles, and beside the front door was a large white ceramic kind of jar—an umbrella stand, maybe, or some sort of ornament—that reminded me of the Parthenon.

Despite this, Emily came down the hallway, bouncing her volleyball as she came.

"Make sure you come back by six o'clock. And watch out for cars," Emily's mother said, stroking Emily on the head.

"Okay, okay. I get it," Emily said with a smile.

I could barely remember the last time my parents had stroked my head, and I felt envious of how loved Emily obviously was.

I never imagined this was the last time Emily and her mother would see each other. And of course I had no idea either that a few hours later I would be back at this house that had me always on pins and needles.

You asked about the day of the murder, but I seem to have talked about everything besides that. I'm not trying to dodge the topic, I'm really not. It's just that whenever I remember the incident my head aches and feels like it's going to break. So as much as I can, I'd like to avoid these heavy topics....

I'll jump ahead to right after we found the body. Is that okay?

Ah, right—maybe I should add this. I think the reason that man didn't take me with him was less that I was heavy than that I'm like a bear.

I think that's about it.... Now I'll get to after we found the body.

So Maki instructed me to run to Emily's—in her stereotypical phrase because I was a *fast runner*—and off I ran. This time I really did race as fast as I could. Yuka and I ran together until we got to the back gate of the school, then each headed off in opposite directions.

Oh my God. This is terrible. Terrible...

My head was filled with these thoughts, but I didn't feel so scared. I think at this point I hadn't grasped the immensity of what had taken place. If I'd considered things a little more carefully, I think I would have gathered my wits and, before I arrived at her house, thought of the best way to inform Emily's mother of the awful reality of her daughter's death. I might have gone home to my house first and had my mother come with me, get help from an adult, might have realized I didn't need to directly use the word *dead*.

But all I did was keep on running for all I was worth.

I was so intent on running, I didn't even notice my brother as I raced past the cigarette shop. At the apartment building, the same property manager was there, but I whizzed right by him and leaped into the elevator.

I arrived at Emily's apartment, ran right up to the intercom, and kept on pushing the button.

"What in the world? You should mind your manners."

Emily's mother said this as she opened the door. Then when she saw me she said, "Oh, Akiko," in a dazed voice. And I stood there, out of breath, and for a split second I thought what a cute flowered apron she had on, then shook my head to gather myself and yelled out as loudly as I could.

"Emily's dead! Emily's dead! Emily's dead!"

The worst possible way to have told her, right? At first she seemed to think it was a joke. Staring at me, she let out a small sigh and, hands on hips, and facing outside the open door, said, "Emily, I know you're hiding there. Stop fooling around and come out. Unless you want to go without dinner."

But Emily wasn't about to come out.

"Emily!"

Once again her mother yelled to her out the door, but the apartment building, with most people gone for the Obon holidays, was quiet, not a sound to be heard.

Emily's mother looked at me, expressionless, for three seconds, five, ten.... Or maybe it was just an instant, I don't know.

"Where is Emily?" she asked, her voice dry and husky.

"At the school swimming pool." My voice was husky too.

"Why Emily?"

An earsplitting voice shot right through my head and I was sent flying. Emily's mother had pushed me aside with both hands and run out of the apartment. My face was knocked against the wall, hard. I fell forward, and with a dull *bang* a sharp pain ran through my forehead. The Parthenon had broken.

Probably because I'd hit my face, my nose was bleeding. Pain in my forehead and a bleeding nose . . . I was sure my skull was cracked and that was where the blood was coming from. The blood ran down my chin, down my neck, flowing profusely. *I might die—help me!* . . . My neck jerked downward and I was struck by the sight of my brand-new blouse, dyed dark red now. *Nooooooo* . . . I felt as if I'd sunk down into a deep, dark hole. And right then—

"Akiko!" a forceful voice called out. I was rescued at the last moment from falling forever into that pit by my brother.

"Koji! Koji!"

I clung to my brother and bawled my eyes out.

My brother had been on his way home from a friend's, and even though Mother had told me to be back by six, since an older cousin would be coming over, when "Greensleeves" had played at six he'd seen me racing off in the opposite direction from our house. So he'd gone off in search of me to call me home. He'd seen Emily's mother dashing out of her building, hair disheveled, and thinking something had to be up, he'd come over here to see what was the matter.

My brother borrowed a wet towel and tissue paper from the property manager and wiped the blood from my nose.

"Am I going to die?" I asked grimly, but my brother only smiled.

"Nobody dies of a nosebleed," he said.

"But my head aches."

"Yeah, your forehead's cut a little. But there's not much blood so it's not so bad."

Finally I was able to stand up. Seeing the shattered Parthenon, he said, "What happened?"

"Emily died at the pool," I replied.

He looked shocked but said, "Let's go home," and gently took my hand.

As we walked down the slope I looked up and saw that the sky was dyed a deep red.

The wound? As you can see, there's no scar.

My brother applied some disinfectant and an adhesive bandage, that's all.

When we came home and my mother saw me covered in blood she let out a scream, but when I told her what had happened she said, "I'm going to the school," and ran off, leaving me behind. She's the kind of person who flies into an instant panic. I heard about this later on, but even though I was right there, standing in front of her eyes, she was convinced it was me who had died at the school.

So despite the pain, the cut had stopped bleeding and it wasn't very deep so I didn't go to the hospital.

Still, even after fifteen years, whenever it rains or is really humid, or when I remember the murder, my forehead aches, and bit by bit I get a splitting headache. Today it's raining, plus

I've been talking so long about the murder, and I feel as if it's going to start soon.

It's already started to ache.

Is that enough about the murder? Hm? The murderer's face? Could you forgive me for not saying anything about that?

All four of us said we *don't remember his face.*

Actually, it's not just his face, but my memory of the whole thing is kind of vague. It's less that I don't remember than, as I said before, whenever I try to recall the murder, especially something really important, my head feels as if it's going to split open. The pain is intolerable. Once I tried to grit my teeth and remember everything, and just as a vague image of the man started to emerge, I was hit by such an overwhelming pain I was sure that if I went any further I'd go mad. So I gave up.

Do you think I should have told the police that when they questioned me?

If I'd said my head hurt, since I still had a bandage on my forehead I felt as if the police and other people would find out that Emily's mother had shoved me, and I hesitated to do that.

The police questioned me several times. They asked the same thing each time, and the first time I went along with what the other three girls had said, so from the second time I answered as if what the others had said was my own memory of events. Maki sometimes used English words—mixing up *green* and *gray*—so I wasn't sure which color the man's work clothes were, but I don't think anybody realized what had happened between me and Emily's mother.

I didn't go into much detail about what had happened at

Emily's house right after the murder, and the police didn't question me about it very much. I didn't even tell my brother about Emily's mother shoving me aside like that. People might have blamed Emily's mother then, and that would have been cruel. Anybody would have flown into a panic if they'd just heard their child had died. It was my fault I got hurt. I shouldn't have been standing there clumsily blocking the door. So when they asked about my injury I told them I was rushing and fell down. Nobody doubted this, since it happened right after we discovered the body.

But more than my own injury, don't you think that Parthenon-like ornament being broken was tens of thousands of times a bigger loss? You know, I hadn't thought of this until now, but maybe the stinging I get sometimes is from a fragment of the ornament that got lodged in my forehead. It certainly feels that way. Too late to take it out now, though. Still, even if I'd known at the time that a porcelain fragment remained in my forehead, I doubt I would have gone to the hospital.

I mean, bears don't go to hospitals, do they? There are vet clinics, of course, but a bear wouldn't go to one on its own, would it?

A bear knows the way a bear's supposed to live. The one who didn't know that was me.

You have to know your station in life.

I've heard my grandfather say this ever since I can remember.

You shouldn't think that everyone's equal. Because some people are given different things from the time they're born.

The poor shouldn't try to act like the rich. A stupid person shouldn't try to act like he's a scholar. A poor person should find happiness in frugality, and a stupid person do his best with what he's capable of. Seek something above your station and it will only lead to sorrow. God is carefully watching us all and will punish you if you reach too high.

My grandfather always ended there, but one day when I was in third grade he added the following:

"So, Akiko, that's why you shouldn't care about being plain-looking."

Can you believe it? Where did that come from? Maybe he said it to make me feel better, but don't you think a statement like that would have the opposite effect? I was big and sturdy, that was true, but I'd never thought my face was that bad. And though I wasn't good at schoolwork, at least I was athletic. Most of the other kids around me weren't much different, so I'd never thought life was unfair. So when my grandfather said that, I just thought *There he goes again!* and didn't pay much attention.

It was only after Emily moved to town that I began to understand what he meant. She was beautiful, with a cute figure, and was smart, athletic, clever, rich. It really wasn't fair. If I compared myself to her I'd feel miserable, but if I put it down to the two of us simply having been given different gifts, it didn't bother me so much. Emily had her life, I had mine. I don't know how the other kids felt about her, but from the first I liked her because she was from a totally different world.

But that day I felt different. I was wearing a cute designer-brand blouse that Emily envied me for, and was happy that my parents had said the same thing to me her parents had said to her. I wanted to be even better friends with her.

I tried to reach beyond my station, and punishment came crashing down.

My Pink House blouse was proof of that. We sent it out to the cleaners, but the brown bloodstains remained and I could never wear it outside again. *Some cute girl might have worn you and taken good care of you,* I told the blouse, *but because a bear who didn't know her place did, all it took was one day to permanently stain you and ruin you. I am so very sorry,* I apologized to the blouse. I clutched it to me, crying and apologizing over and over. *Forgive me... forgive me....*

And Emily—*forgive me. Please forgive me,* I said.

Because a bear like me, who should have known better, wanted to be friends with a girl like you. That's why you were murdered.

My life after the murder? Seek something above your station and it will only lead to sorrow. Emily was murdered because of me, so how could I go on doing the things I'd done before the murder—going to school, playing with friends, eating sweets, laughing? I felt as if I wasn't allowed to anymore.

Being with people would only cause trouble for them. Even if I didn't have a relationship with a person, it felt as if just my presence alone would cause trouble for anyone I happened to be with.

I was worried that at school, if I moved at all I'd bump into somebody and knock them over and injure them, so except for trips to the restroom during recess I stayed glued to my seat.

Before long I started waking up with an upset stomach, or feeling listless, and would skip school.

My parents and teachers didn't say much about my absences, figuring it was only natural considering what I'd been through in fourth grade, but when I got into fifth they seemed to think enough was enough. Even if a murder takes place in their own town, after half a year people not directly involved see it as some distant, past event.

It was my older brother, Koji, who encouraged me then.

"Akiko," he told me, "it might be scary for you going outside, but I'll protect you, so keep your chin up!"

Koji started walking with me to my school in the morning before going on to his junior high, though it was out of his way. Saying we should both work out so even if a criminal attacked us we could fight him off, he fashioned barbells out of unused farm tools in our shed, and we did weight training together.

Though I felt a guilty conscience about going to school, I enjoyed the training. You'd expect a bear to be strong, and I was really into it, thinking that someday I'd be able to get revenge for Emily.

The days passed and Emily's parents were soon moving back to Tokyo and the four of us were asked over to Emily's place to talk, one more time, about the day of the murder.

Other than the missing Parthenon ornament, the foyer was the same as before, and as soon as I took a step inside my forehead began to sting. But Maki did most of the talking and I was able to get through it.

But then Emily's mother said this:

"I will never forgive you, unless you find the murderer before the statute of limitations is up. If you can't do that, then atone for what you've done, in a way I'll accept. If you don't do either one, I'm telling you here and now—I *will* have revenge on each and every one of you."

It was my fault Emily died, so I felt bad for the other three girls, but I knew from the start that Emily's mother blamed me, so it didn't frighten me to hear she'd take revenge. What seemed strange to me was that she hadn't said anything up till then. I figured finding the murderer would be hard, since I could remember hardly anything about the incident, so I chose to do penance instead.

Penance? *Never reach for anything beyond your station.* This thought never left my head after the murder, and on that day I pledged again to follow that stricture.

I ended up not going on to high school. My parents tried to persuade me to at least graduate from high school, but even if I took the exams I had no confidence I could make it through three more years of school.

My brother was the one who convinced my parents to let me be.

"High school isn't compulsory education," he argued. "If she doesn't want to go outside but still wants to study, she can always still get a GED by correspondence, and then take college entrance exams. I'll go out and be a success, so let Akiko do things at her own pace."

That's what he told them. And true to his word, he graduated from a nearby national university, took the civil service exam, and was hired at the local city hall, where he became a well-respected staff member in the welfare section. People saw him as a wonderful, devoted son, and he made my parents proud.

Koji always liked to help people. That's why the person he married was a woman with a dubious past.

Don't get taken in by some sketchy man, get knocked up, and come back home in tears now.

Kind of a cliché parents and relatives always tell their daughters when they go off to school or to work in the big city, but my brother's wife, Haruka, was a perfect example of all the terrible things that can happen to a woman alone in a city.

She got a job in a printing company in Tokyo but could barely get by on the modest salary this small company paid her, so she started working part-time at a bar to earn some extra spending money. There she got involved with a low-level yakuza. The man got her pregnant but didn't marry her, and she quit the company, had the child, and somehow managed to raise her on what she earned working at bars. Meanwhile, the yakuza guy started seeing another woman and vanished. On top of that, the man had gotten into heavy debt to some shady loan company, and loan sharks threatened her that if she didn't pay it back by the following month they'd put her in concrete and toss her into Tokyo Bay. She barely escaped their clutches and ran back to our town.

It's hard to know how much of this story was true, but a month after Haruka had come back, the whole town knew all the juicy details. Even someone like me, who never ventured outside her home, had heard about it.

I was sitting with my mother and a neighbor woman who'd

come over, and listened in on what she said, just as if I were one of their cronies. In a know-it-all tone the woman reviewed the rumors about Haruka, sounding, though, as if she couldn't believe that Haruka had turned out that way. I found it hard to believe too.

I don't know if it was to pay back those loans, but Haruka's family did sell off some farmland and land they owned in the hills, and it was true that Haruka had a child.

Still, what I found hard to believe was the question of—image, I guess you'd call it? She might be held up as a bad example, but in this town her story took on the outlines of a heroic saga. People who didn't know her were curious to see what kind of beauty could have gotten into such a fix, right? But Haruka was a modest, quiet person, and not really much of a beauty by any standard.

She and Koji were former classmates, and our houses weren't far from each other, so I'd known her since she was a child. At that point I still hadn't seen her since she'd come back from Tokyo, and kind of expected the big city must have turned her into a sophisticated woman. But three months after I heard these rumors about her, my brother brought her over to our house and I found that, though she'd matured, as you'd expect, with the passing of years, she really hadn't changed at all.

This was on Obon last year, on August fourteenth.

Ten years ago my grandfather and grandmother passed away, one after the other, so other relatives don't gather at our place anymore, but on that day one of my older cousins, Seiji—my aunt Yoko's son who'd just come back after five years abroad for work—was coming to stay over with his wife. So my mother and I prepared all kinds of good food—sukiyaki and sushi—and we waited, along with my father, for them to arrive. My brother had been out since morning, and he phoned to say that, with Seiji visiting, he'd like to use the opportunity to introduce us all to his girlfriend.

It was news to me that he had a girlfriend. Same with my mother, who was rattled, wondering whether she should change her clothes, or maybe go out and buy a cake. But when Seiji and his wife arrived my mother shelved that and focused on entertaining my cousin and his wife.

My parents were the only ones from our family who had attended Seiji's wedding in Tokyo eight years before, so I think this was the first time I'd ever actually met Seiji's wife, Misato.

"I'm so happy you would come all this way to the country-side to see us, even though Grandfather and Grandmother are no longer with us," my mother said. To which Seiji replied, a bit apologetically, "Of course we want to pay our respects at their graves, but this place also has a lot of memories for the two of us....

"I know this is an indiscreet thing to say," he continued, "so I've never mentioned it before, but if that incident hadn't taken place we might never have gone out with each other. So we've been hoping to pay a visit here, the two of us, someday."

By *incident* he meant Emily's murder.

Seiji, who'd been a junior in college in Tokyo back then, had been in the tennis club and had had his eye on one of the other members from a women's college, Misato, who was a fresh-man. There were many other rivals for her attention, and he found it hard to shed the role of upperclassman mentor. But one day, when the club members had gone out drinking and they were talking about going back to their hometowns for Obon, Seiji had bragged, "My hometown's got nothing to recommend it, though it does have the cleanest air in Japan," to which Misato said, "I'd like to go there sometime." Misato and her parents were all from Tokyo, and she was enchanted by the idea of going home to the countryside. Spurred on by a few drinks, Seiji said, "Well, would you like to go together?" and Misato smiled and nodded her assent.

Like everyone in our family, Seiji is a serious type who likes to take care of others. Here was a chance to stay overnight with a girl he liked, but the plan he made was, after they ate with us, to just stay over one night in our house and then go straight back to Tokyo. Seiji would stay in my brother's bedroom, Misato in my room. Even I, pretty ignorant of anything to do with love, was surprised that he didn't take advantage of being with the girl he liked.

The two of them arrived at the railroad station just before 6 p.m. and walked to our house, arriving after six. They put down their luggage and took a short rest, then my mother said, "Well, we're all here now, so I'll get the sukiyaki ready." But she couldn't find her children and just as she was complaining, "Now where did the kids get to?" I appeared, my brother leading me by the hand. I hadn't noticed that Seiji and Misato were there.

My mother flew into a panic then and raced out. There were police sirens wailing outside and one of my uncles said, out of curiosity, that he'd go see what was up. By this time the whole West District was in an uproar.

This wasn't the time to be entertaining guests, naturally, and Misato told us not to mind about them. Aunt Yoko booked a place for them in a Japanese inn in a nearby town and Seiji and Misato moved over there. This nearby town isn't much of a place, but it does have hot springs, and with the crowds home for Obon only one room in the inn was available.

Misato was understandably shaken by the news that a murder had just taken place in this country town she was visiting for the first time, but Seiji told her, "Don't worry, I'll protect you," which she found comforting, and that was really the start of their relationship. I think that even if the murder hadn't happened they would have gotten together. I mean, no matter how clean the air might be, or how much a person might want to visit the countryside for the holiday, do you really think she would go to the house of the relatives of someone she didn't even like? But I would agree that the murder heightened their feelings for each other.

Fast-forward fourteen years. I don't know the reasons, but Seiji and Misato didn't have any children. But eight years had passed since their marriage and I envied how much like newlywed lovers they remained.

As I watched how close they were my mother said, buoyantly, "Koji's bringing a girl over today." Koji was her pride and joy, and having him bring a girl over to visit had her all excited. Maybe, seeing Seiji and his wife, she was thinking how much she wanted Koji, too, to have a happy marriage.

Seiji and Misato were just saying they wondered what kind of person Koji's girlfriend was and how they looked forward to meeting her when Koji appeared. With Haruka and Wakaba, too.

Wakaba is Haruka's daughter. She was in second grade then.

Mother greeted them pleasantly and showed them into the living room. She then took me into the kitchen and said, "It's…it's—*her*, right?" Meaning that the woman he'd brought home to meet us was none other than the Haruka everyone was whispering about. I was pretty surprised myself, but seeing Mother pace back and forth in the kitchen in a panic, it actually made me calmer.

"Yes, that's her, all right. But they're former classmates, so maybe that's all it is. Don't get so worked up. It's rude."

I gave Mother a nudge and she went back to the living room with a bottle of juice and as many bottles of beer as she could carry.

I thought my father was downing the beers a bit faster than usual, but this was because of Seiji and his wife being there, and dinner proceeded smoothly. Haruka sat modestly next to Koji, almost hiding behind his large frame, and barely ate a bite, though she was very attentive, pouring beer for the others, serving them sushi, stacking the empty plates up.

If I'd done the same thing it would have been so slow and inefficient that someone would have told me to stop "helping," but Haruka did it all so naturally and unobtrusively you almost didn't notice. She had on what was no doubt her best outfit, but it was the cheap kind you could buy in a supermarket in the next town over. As if I should talk—my usual outfit was a brown sweatshirt and sweatpants.

Watching Haruka, I felt as if she'd lived her whole life here, and that the rumors were just so much nonsense.

At first my mother acted sulky, serving up the sukiyaki without a word, but when Wakaba told her "Thank you!" with a cute smile when Mother broke a raw egg into her bowl for her, Mother finally smiled herself and made sure the little girl got plenty of meat to eat. When he saw this, my father said, apropos of nothing, "I can break an egg with one hand, you know," breaking an egg into a bowl. When Father saw how happy this made Wakaba, he told me to go out to the mini-mart and buy some ice cream for her.

This was the only mini-mart in town, built three years before near the elementary school. Seiji said he'd run out of cigarettes and went with me.

"Is Koji thinking of marrying that woman?" Seiji asked me along the way.

"I kind of doubt it…"

"Makes sense. She seems okay, but it'd be better if he didn't."

It was kind of strange that Seiji, who knew nothing about Haruka's background, would have that sort of strong opinion. If I had only known her from this one evening, I think I would have welcomed the match. "How come?" I asked Seiji, but he came out with a loud "Wow! Get a load of this!"

"What's with this parking lot?" he asked. "It's three times bigger than the whole store!"

So what? I wondered. I couldn't figure it out. *Seiji was raised in the big city, and there's a ton of things he says that I just don't get,* I was thinking as we went inside the mini-mart.

Seeing all the local people crowding the place, Seiji said, "This has to be the most popular spot in town." He sounded impressed. He bought the ice cream, some snacks that would go well with sake, cigarettes, and the kind of weekly magazine that office workers read, and the two of us headed back the way we'd come.

Seiji didn't say anything more about Koji. What did we talk about on the way back? ... Seiji was silent, smoking as we walked, and then suddenly he asked about the murder. Nothing all that important, I think. I don't recall my forehead starting to ache or anything....

"Akiko, that murderer was the same pervert who stole dolls on the night of the festival, right?" he asked.

I just replied, "That's right."

We never displayed any French dolls in our house. Instead, we had a carved wooden bear, a memento from Hokkaido. So until he brought it up, the whole incident of the stolen French dolls had totally slipped my mind.

Dinner ended up more amiably than I had expected, so I think Koji misjudged the situation. The next morning, after breakfast, when Seiji, his wife, and we were all having some coffee, talking about going to the hot springs in the town next door, Koji suddenly blurted out:

"Mom, Dad—Haruka and I are going to get married."

He wasn't asking permission but declaring his intention.

"Don't be stupid!" Mother yelled. She stood up, pointlessly, then sat down again, obviously in a panic.

"How can you think of marrying a person like her?" she shouted. "There are so many better women out there you could marry. Like the Yamagatas' daughter, who works in the lab at Adachi Manufacturing, the one who went to the same college you did. And then the Kawanos' girl, who went to music college and teaches piano. Both of them would like to marry you, so why in the world do you want to marry *that* kind of woman?"

Small point of correction, but it was the girls' parents who wanted them to marry Koji, not the girls themselves. The neighbor woman who gossiped all about Haruka when she came had actually come to our place to sound out Koji about another possible match. At the time Koji had told her, "I'm not going to marry until I'm thirty."

"You're the only one we can count on to carry on after we're gone. Don't be carried away by some infatuation!" my father yelled too.

It hurt me a little for him to imply that if I weren't the way I am he wouldn't have opposed the marriage, but more than that, I felt apologetic to my brother. Koji had always taken care of me, but here he was unable to marry the person he loved because of me. Haruka's past worried me, but I felt that if I was ever to repay my brother the time was now.

"I don't think...that Haruka's such a bad person," I said. "And I'll take care of you, Mom and Dad, when you're old...."

"Don't be ridiculous. This isn't the time for a recluse like you to interrupt. I don't expect a thing from you. As long as you don't bother others, that's all we can ask for. So don't butt in."

This was from my mother. She was right, but no one had ever put it this clearly before. I'd been so excited about having guests over—we so rarely did—and had half forgotten my status as a lumbering bear.

"Seiji, *say* something to him," Mother added. "And Misato—don't you think there's something not right about that woman?" And she started filling them in on all the rumors about Haruka.

She didn't need to say this in front of Koji, I was thinking, but what surprised me was that Koji didn't deny any of it. In fact, when Seiji asked, "Is all this true, Koji?" my brother silently nodded. And then he said this:

"I feel sorry for Haruka. Ms. Yamagata or Ms. Kawano can be happy with anybody. But the only one in the entire world who can make Haruka happy is me. If you insist on opposing us, then I'll take Haruka and Wakaba and leave town."

He spoke quietly but forcefully. My brother had met Haruka again at the service counter at city hall, where he worked. She'd come to apply for support for single mothers and Koji was manning the counter that day. I'm just guessing here, but my brother, always the type to help others, must have done his utmost to advise her, first as a member of the welfare section of city hall, then as a former classmate. Eventually he'd found himself wanting to protect her as a man.

Father sat there stolidly, not uttering a word. Mother's mouth quivered like a fish gasping for breath. Seiji and Misato were silent, staring at Koji. And I...sat there vacantly thinking, *Ah, so Koji and Haruka's marriage is decided.* I looked around at everyone and felt a large hand come to rest on my head.

"Thank you, Akiko, for being on my side." As he said this,

Koji slowly stroked my head, and tears welled up and I couldn't stop them. That may have been the first time since the murder that I'd cried.

The following month, the beginning of September, Koji officially registered Haruka as his wife. The wedding ceremony was held at a nearby Buddhist temple with just relatives present, and struck me as more like a dressed-up memorial service, but Koji and Haruka seemed very happy. People in town at first wondered why he would marry a woman like that, but Haruka's parents were decent, upstanding people, Haruka herself was quiet, reserved, and polite, and gradually people started to wish them well. And Koji had an even higher reputation in town, people seeing him now as a man of real character.

Hoping to one day build a home that two generations could live in together, Koji and Haruka rented a unit in a two-story building a ten-minute walk from our house. It wasn't so tall a building but on the outside was as chic-looking as the Adachi Manufacturing apartment complex.

As soon as Haruka was officially in the family register as Koji's wife, my parents' attitude did an abrupt about-face. Perhaps happy that a cute little girl now graced their dowdy home, they'd use any silly excuse—that they'd just gotten some fresh grapes or apples, for instance—to invite Wakaba over and then take her out to the mini-mart to buy whatever sweets or drinks she liked.

Wakaba became very attached to me. One day when she came to visit she seemed unusually dejected, and when I asked her why she replied, "I can't jump rope." *Jump rope*—now, that brought back memories. "Would you like to practice in our yard?" I asked, and she went home and came back with a pink jump rope. They'd bought it for her but she'd never had the length adjusted. It was too long for her, but since she'd gone to the trouble of bringing it over, I decided to demonstrate how to jump rope before we cut it shorter.

Leaping jump, jogging step, crossover step, double hop, double crossover...I hadn't jumped rope in over ten years and at first kept getting tangled up, but five minutes was all it took to get the feeling back. Did I get out of breath? No way. I mean, I still spent half of each day doing weight training. So there was no way a little jumping rope would tire me out.

"Akiko, you're great!" Wakaba shouted happily. I think she found it interesting that someone as visibly bulky as me was jumping around so lightly. After that she came to practice almost every day after school. I bought a matching jump rope for myself at the mini-mart and we practiced together.

"Hang in there! Just a little more! I know you can do it, Wakaba!" I told her.

Wakaba practiced until it got dark, and then my mother always invited her to eat dinner with us, preparing the kinds of dishes that would make a child happy, but Wakaba never ate with us. "Yay!" she'd say excitedly. "You mean I can eat with all of you?" But Haruka would always come to take her home before she could.

Mother invited Haruka to eat with us, but she always declined. Even though she knew it would end up like this, Mother still prepared kids' favorites like hamburgers and fried shrimp, and as she watched frumpy old Father and me chomping away

by ourselves, she never voiced any complaints. I think it's because of how skillful Haruka was in turning down her offers:
"I'd like to wait until Koji comes home," she'd say, "and then
the three of us eat dinner together. Because Wakaba loves her
daddy."

One mention of my brother and there was nothing Mother
could say. Also, from time to time Haruka would invite my
parents and me to dinner with them. As I said, they lived
close to our house, but I thought she was really an amazing
daughter-in-law to invite her in-laws for dinner even though it
wasn't anyone's birthday or anything.

At dinner my brother would enjoy some beers and talk
about things, like when he went with Wakaba on a school
outing to help harvest rice. He seemed really happy, though
one thing bothered me. The only dishes Haruka ever made
were ones geared to a child's tastes. At home we'd always
eaten mostly Japanese dishes. Not just because Grandfather
and Grandmother lived with us. It was because all of us, Koji
included, preferred the plain, simple taste of Japanese food.

I figured Haruka should have at least prepared one dish
that Koji liked, but everything was geared to Wakaba. Maybe
when she saw my mother making children's dishes every night,
Haruka mistakenly thought that was the kind of food our family liked. The idea did cross my mind.

"Come stay with us over the weekend, Wakaba," my
mother said. "Let Mommy and Daddy be alone, just the two
of them sometimes. They're still newlyweds, after all. And you
want to have a baby brother or sister someday, don't you?"

Mother didn't seem to mind the menu Haruka had made,

happily reaching for the curry-flavored chicken nuggets. She loved little Wakaba, but I'm sure she hoped to have a grandchild of her own as soon as she could.

"You shouldn't talk like that in front of a child," my brother said, scolding her, though he didn't seem too upset. Once when he'd stopped by our house he spotted his childhood baseball glove and said how he'd love to have a son someday. However...

"I'm not so sure about that. Wakaba tosses and turns all night." Haruka seemed genuinely concerned. "I might kick Akiko in the tummy," Wakaba added playfully. The atmosphere then was quite friendly and warm, but in the end Wakaba never did come to stay overnight with us.

Even after she went into third grade and was already proficient at jump rope, Wakaba still stopped over often at our house. This time she came to practice doing flips on the horizontal bar. We didn't have a bar at our house, so we went to a nearby park to practice. A forward flip? Of course I can do it. I can do it many times in a row, without kicking my legs, just keeping them straight. 'Cause I trained specially to, when I was a kid.

Time passed, and after the holidays in May something happened that took me by surprise.

Haruka gave me a present of some beautiful shoes. "This is for always taking care of Wakaba for me," she said. During the holidays she, Koji, and Wakaba had gone to a department store in the city and had bought them there.

These were designer sneakers, not made by a sporting goods company but by a women's shoe company, with a pink and beige leather patchwork design. Pretty little shoes a world apart from the cheap canvas shoes I normally bought at a supermarket.

"I have this, too, for you, if it's all right," Haruka said, and gave me a pair of jeans. "I bought these," she said, "but I have a pretty large rear end and don't look good in them, so I've hardly worn them." Haruka is so slim, though, I was sure they wouldn't fit me.

"Akiko," she continued, "you have wide shoulders, and your upper body is pretty solidly built, but your legs are slim and very attractive. And your behind is tight, so it's really a waste for you to wear such loose-fitting pants. I'm sorry, I know I'm being kind of forward. It's just that I envy you."

Far from ever comparing my own legs to anybody else's, I'd never even really examined them closely. But since she was nice enough to give me the jeans, I took off my brown sweatpants and, lo and behold, found they fit my legs perfectly. They might have been a tad short, but if I wore them with the cute shoes it might be better for them to be on the short side.

When Mother came back from taking Wakaba to the minimart she was surprised to see this outfit on me. "Come to think of it…," she said, and got out a black Hard Rock Cafe T-shirt, a souvenir a neighbor had bought on her honeymoon as a present for her, but that Mother had been too shy to ever wear. When I put that on, Wakaba said, clapping her hands, "Akiko, you look cool!"

What stood out now was my loose, disheveled hair, held back in a ponytail with a rubber band. Haruka introduced me to a beauty parlor in the next town, where a friend of hers worked. I went there with Wakaba, who wanted to get a trim. Going to a real beauty parlor, not a barbershop, was a first for me, as was riding with Wakaba, just the two of us, on a train.

I'm still not sure what they mean by *teasing out* the ends of one's hair, but they cut my hair short in a casual-looking style, and evened up my eyebrows, too. Koji had given me some extra spending money, encouraging us to have something nice to eat before coming back, and Wakaba and I enjoyed some sweets at a coffee shop near the station.

As I ate the tart, which had some kind of strawberryish fruits on top whose name I didn't know, Wakaba watched me closely.

"You're really cool-looking, Akiko," she said. "Mom told me it would be nice if I had been born a boy, but I think you would look even better as a boy than me."

"Really? She said that? But if I were a boy, then I would be your older brother or your father."

"Oh, right…"

"Do you like your papa?"

"Uh-huh, a lot. He came on the outing to plant rice plants, and helps me with my homework. He's so nice. The other day I kicked him in the middle of the night and he didn't get angry at all."

"Hm? You sleep in the same room?"

"Uh-huh. I sleep in the middle between them. Mama says that parents who get along well sleep like that."

Wakaba sounded really happy as she said this. I'd always thought she must sleep in a separate room, but a third grader is still a pretty young child, and I'd slept in the same room with

my brother until I was in fourth grade, so I didn't find it so unusual.

One day in the middle of June Haruka's mother collapsed
while working their farm and was hospitalized in the city.
Haruka was an only child, so she went to take care of her
mother, and we took care of Wakaba while she was away.

Still, Wakaba never stayed overnight with us. It was a two-
hour trip by train each way to the hospital, and Mother thought
Wakaba should stay with us and that Haruka should sleep at
the hospital. But Haruka insisted on coming home each day.

She said she couldn't stand being apart from Koji and Wakaba.

Mother told me, on the quiet, that she feared Haruka had
some mental issues. Since she'd been abused by that yakuza
guy in Tokyo, even now, when she was living a happy life, she
might still be afraid that if she took her eyes off her daughter
she would disappear.

I told Mother I was impressed by the way she made those
connections, and she said a similar scenario had played out on a
Korean TV drama. I could see that. We decided we'd do whatever we could to keep Haruka from worrying too much.

Wakaba came straight to our house right after school let out
and did her homework, and then we'd practice like always on
the horizontal bars and toss a ball around. Then Koji would
drop by after work, we'd all have dinner, and after Wakaba had
had a bath she would go back to their apartment with him.

Mother prepared kid-friendly dishes especially for Wakaba
but was happy to see Wakaba gobbling down the *Chikuzen-ni*

soy-cooked vegetables on a plate in the middle of the table—
"*Delicious!*" Wakaba said—and after that Mother made more
of the Japanese-style dishes she was good at. I was surprised
when Wakaba said she didn't know *nikujaga*, a common meat-
and-potatoes Japanese dish.

I was thinking maybe Haruka wasn't good at cooking. Yet
the Western-style dishes she made when she invited us over
had that special touch and were very tasty, so now I rethought
things and decided that Haruka simply preferred Western-
style food.

Like a typical overly indulgent grandfather, my father
bought tons of sweets for Wakaba every day, which Koji
scolded him for, and when in the second-term PE class at
school they were going to learn to ride a unicycle, my father
bought her one.

I helped her with her homework, and though she managed
to get by in arithmetic, it was kind of pathetic the way she
could never remember Chinese characters. After we finished
homework we'd practice her unicycle and then take a bath together.

I'd never ridden a unicycle before either, and we'd go to the
park and practice, having a ball until it got dark. Strictly speaking she was my stepniece, not a blood relation, but the truth
was Wakaba was my one and only friend.

And then things started to change.

It was the beginning of July, about two weeks after Wakaba and I started taking baths together, that I first discovered
bruises on her body. Her waist was red and puffy and I asked
her what had happened. She looked down. "I don't know"

was all she said. "Maybe it was the unicycle," she said after a while.

I had the same kind of bruises on my knees, so I believed her.

It was a week later, one evening just before summer vacation, when I found out the real reason for her bruises.

The town was abuzz with news about Sae having killed her husband, and about Maki getting caught up in that terrible attack on her students. This town is cursed, people said. It's been fifteen years since TV crews came here, but suddenly they said—"Hold on! Weren't both of them playing with that girl who was murdered back then? The murderer hasn't been caught yet. What *is* all this?" Little by little it seemed like people in town started to recall Emily's murder and all that had happened.

Apparently there were phone calls to city hall suggesting that they ask TV programs to do an investigation, since the statute of limitations was due to run out soon. "Why on earth does the city hall have to do that?" my brother complained over dinner. "Both women live somewhere else. It's just a coincidence. Akiko's living a normal life, and if people start all kinds of groundless speculation, it's annoying."

He turned to Wakaba beside him and gently cautioned her: "If a stranger talks to you, never go with him. Mommy and Daddy have to be really careful," he said to her, "since you're so cute, Wakaba." He ignored me and was only worried about Wakaba. That wasn't necessarily the reason, but I decided not to say anything about getting two letters from Emily's mother.

After I got the letters my forehead started aching and wouldn't let up.

What did the letters say? I was too scared to read them. I didn't even open them. They were sent, one soon after the other, right before the statute of limitations was going to run out, so I'm sure the point was to remind me of the murder one more time. They're in my desk drawer in my room, so if you'd like to read them, feel free.

And on top of that same desk...after Wakaba had finished her homework and had gone home with my brother, I noticed she'd forgotten a homework handout and her key to her apartment.

In the mornings Wakaba went directly to school without stopping by our place, and though it was raining I decided to go over to their place that evening to return the handout and key. It was about 10 p.m. I heard that Haruka came home every night around eleven, and I thought I'd give them to Koji after Wakaba was asleep.

Their bedroom was on the first floor in the very back. I should have gone to the front door and rung the intercom, but I'd cut across the parking lot in back and had seen the light on in the kitchen, which faced outside, and the window was open a crack and I thought about calling in through there and having Koji take the items Wakaba had forgotten.

But when I peeked in through the opening I didn't see anyone in the kitchen. I was about to go around to the front door when I heard a small voice from the room in back.

"*Help!*" the voice said.

What's going on? I wondered. Was Wakaba feeling sick?

"Are you okay?" I was about to call into the open window, when I heard a different voice.

"Don't be afraid. It feels better now, doesn't it? This is a kind of ceremony so we can really become parent and child. Parents and children who get along well always do this together."

The ache in my forehead quickly spread to my entire head. It felt as if it was going to split apart. I didn't understand what was going on, but a feeling of disgust rose up inside me...the exact same feeling I had when we found Emily's dead body. I should never have opened that door. I remembered how much I regretted doing so years before.

I turned my back on the window, determined to leave before my head hurt even more, but just then I heard that voice again calling out for help. And that other voice.

"You always behave. Why not today? Who are you calling to for help? Aren't I the one who helped you?"

She was calling to me for help. What should I do? ... Frightened, I shut my eyes tight, and when I did a voice echoed in my head.

Hang in there! Just a little more! I know you can do it, Akiko!

I have to do it. This is why I've trained every day.

For this moment.

I opened my eyes, took a deep breath, and, using the forgotten key, opened the front door and quietly slipped inside. I stepped softly, heading for the room the voices were coming from, and yanked open the door.

And there I found a bear.

In the dark room, lit only by the light filtering in from

the kitchen, a bear lay heavily on top of a naked little girl. As I stood there silently, the bear slowly lifted his head. I'd pictured an awful, scary face, but what I saw instead was a relaxed, genial-looking face. Within the bear's shadows, I caught a glimpse of the girl's face.

It was—Emily.

Crying, she looked up at me.

Emily was being attacked. But she wasn't dead. *Thank God—I'm in time!* The criminal was a bear. *I have to help Emily. Help her this very instant. Otherwise—she'll be strangled and killed.*

In a corner of the room, next to a little backpack, was the jump rope. I grabbed it, untied it, and wrapped it around the neck of the bear, still pressed down on Emily. He looked about to start crying, and I yanked it as hard as I could. The bear's eyes, startled, went wide and he struggled, but I tightened the rope with all my might and with a thud he toppled over on top of Emily and lay there, unmoving.

At the same instant, Emily's cries rang out through the room.

Thank God, I rescued her. I'll go get Emily's mother to come and take her home.

I turned around, and standing there, right in front of me, was Emily's mother.

Oh, I see. She was worried and came to get Emily.

Emily's mother stood there, silent and dazed, staring at the collapsed bear.

"It was touch and go," I said to her eagerly, "but I saved her. 'Cause I'm so strong."

I was sure Emily's mother would thank me and stroke my hair. And then I would be freed from this awful pain, my head splitting as if my brain were going to be ground to powder and blow away...

I waited expectantly, but what I heard were different words entirely.

"Why couldn't you mind your own business..."

At that instant I heard the sound of something collapsing.

It was Wakaba who had been attacked. Wakaba whom the bear was assaulting. And I had killed the bear. Was this—a crime? Maybe it was—

When you said you wanted to hear about the murder, was it this one you meant?

Then you should have told me earlier.

I heard that Wakaba was put in an orphanage facility. Again sounding as if she was mimicking a Korean TV drama, Mother said that Haruka was to blame for everything. Because she had never loved my brother at all. Even so, she had accepted his proposal because marrying him seemed like the easiest way to turn around her messed-up life.

Even if she didn't love him, once they married she should have done her wifely duty, but she didn't allow Koji to ever touch her. She must not have wanted another child. It must have been the aftereffects of the violence she'd suffered from that yakuza guy. Not being able to stay anywhere overnight, and only being able to cook the dishes that man liked, were all due to the trauma of that earlier time. She must have been quite traumatized. But still, if only she had talked with us about it...

Instead, she chose the cruelest method of all.

She wanted a peaceful life but didn't want a man—my brother—to ever touch her. So she offered up Wakaba. Koji couldn't have been hoping for that. If she had opened up to him I know he would have understood. But step by step Haruka drove Koji to it. Completely ignoring what it would do to her very own daughter, her own flesh and blood... Who knows, maybe Haruka wasn't even aware she was suffering from the aftereffects of trauma.

Wakaba was lovely—pale skin, chiseled features, slim long arms and legs. The very image of her yakuza father, apparently. But for Haruka, Wakaba was nothing more than a tool she used to find her own happiness.

Whenever Wakaba came up in the conversation it always made my mother cry. We can't ever see her again, but she is alive. The children's home is in our prefecture, I heard, so who knows, someday, somewhere, I might run into her.

And that would be enough. Enough for a bear family. That incident wasn't Haruka's fault. We'd forgotten what our grandfather had taught us, had tried to reach for something above our station in life, and were punished for it. If only Koji had not been so prideful as to think that he alone could make an unhappy person happy, and had married a healthy, straight-forward person who would make a good companion for a bear, they would have been blessed with a cute child. And then everyone could have taken good care of that child. Because no one had a problem having a cute little girl come to a bear's house, they were overjoyed by it, in fact. That's why no one noticed what was really going on.

No—Seiji knew. He'd told us it was better for Koji not to marry her. If only he had made his case more forcefully.

But the real one to blame is *me*.

I should have known long ago something was wrong.... I've spent the last fifteen years thinking of nothing else.... Instead I wore those cute shoes, went to a beauty parlor, ate a tart, and became this little girl's friend.

If Emily's mother knew all this, she would definitely take revenge. Probably shoot the bear. She's rich, so I bet she owns a gun.

I'm not afraid, just wondering if there's anything else I can say that would be helpful.

Oh—one more thing.

This was last year when Seiji stayed at our house. In the middle of the night as I was passing by the guest room on the way to the toilet, I overheard him say to Misato:

"Do you remember fourteen years ago, Misato, when we arrived at the station? You turned around to look at a man you'd just passed, and I was sort of jealous and said, 'Hm—so you like *that* type, huh?' and you said, 'He looks like a teacher I had in elementary school.' Isn't this the guy?"

I heard the sound of pages in a magazine being flipped open. And then Misato said:

"That's him. I remember now. I was wondering: *Why is Mr. Nanjo in a place like this?* Because I'd heard there was an accident and he quit teaching and moved to the Kansai area. A boy in his free school had set a fire. I'm sure that was him. It's hard to think he'd run a place like that. But then again, he was always such a fine teacher, with a strong sense of duty."

Could this be a clue? I mean, Misato saw someone she never expected to see here, right? What if he were the murderer? ... Oh, that's right—I forgot about the French doll affair. The pervert who stole the French dolls was the one who murdered Emily. That's why Seiji asked me about it on the way back from the mini-mart....

Someone who lives in Kansai, even farther away than Tokyo, isn't going to come all the way to this town to steal French dolls, is he....

So it's too late. And there are only five more days until the statute of limitations runs out.

I wanted to ask—are you really a professional counselor? You remind me more and more of Emily's mother.... But I'm just imagining things, I suppose.

I'm sorry, but my head is splitting. Can I go home now? It's still raining a little. I'd like them to come get me, but I don't have a cell phone, so could you call them for me? I don't have the cell phone number on me, it's at home.... Call the welfare section at city hall, if you would.

Ten Months and Ten Days

My contractions are still twenty minutes apart so it looks like they won't let me into the standby room quite yet. So could we talk here, if you don't mind? I know—a waiting room in a big hospital in the middle of the night is dark and kind of creepy, but no one will bother us, so it might actually be a good place to talk about that incident. There's a vending machine, too. But I was wondering—have you ever had canned coffee from a machine?

Really? You like it? I never would have guessed.

There are five other women here tonight with contractions ten minutes apart, so the staff is kind of busy. The nurse had this sour look on her face and told me, "You didn't need to come here yet...." I didn't plan to come here this early myself, and just basically stopped by to say hello, but don't you think that was rude of her? I thought giving birth was supposed to be a more sacred event, something people should appreciate more. Especially with the declining birth rate in this region.

It wasn't this crowded when I came in for my last checkup, and I wonder why it is tonight of all nights. I always feel as if I'm an extra in life, but I never imagined that when it came to giving birth I'd be treated as if I'm on an assembly line. Just my luck.

My due date is still a little way off, and at my checkup last week I was told the baby might be a little late, but today I went out at night, which I don't do a lot, and maybe the waxing and waning of the moon had an impact. I hear it often does.

My due date is August fourteenth.

A year has 365 days, so doesn't it make you wonder why this day of all days? Just one day earlier or later would be enough, but that's the day the doctor said, so there's nothing I can do about it.

A surprising number of people don't know how to accurately calculate the normal gestation period. The notion of *ten months and ten days* that people talk about is, to begin with, wrong....

For example, say your doctor tells you your due date is October tenth, then most people would simply subtract ten months and ten days and figure it was January first when the couple had intercourse. But that's not the case. You don't figure the due date as *ten months and ten days* from the time you had sex, but rather forty weeks, or 280 days, from the start of your last period. It's a bit complicated, but what you do is subtract three from the month when your last period started. If you can't subtract three, then add nine, then add seven to the day when your last period started.

So in the example I gave, the day the last period started would be January third, so the sex that led to the pregnancy would most likely be between January fifteenth and the nineteenth—counting one week for the period and one week afterward for ovulation.

You've given birth, so I know I don't need to explain this to you. Most people don't really care about figuring exactly which act of intercourse led to their pregnancy, but a friend of mine from high school, Yamagata, nearly got divorced because of this.

Yamagata got married to a man who is a serious and conscientious type, and when she showed signs of being pregnant she went to the hospital and was told she was three months pregnant. She happily reported this to her husband. Her husband was overjoyed too, and circled the due date on the calendar. But when he flipped back through the calendar *ten months and ten days* to calculate when the child had been conceived, he saw it was when he'd been on a business trip. And that's when he started to have his doubts.

"Are you sure it's my child?" he demanded. "Did you have an affair when I was out of town?" He started to press Yamagata, insisting on her showing him her cell phone, and things quickly escalated. For her part she'd simply been told the due date and didn't know the correct way of calculating conception, so she couldn't explain it away easily. *"I never, ever had an affair!"* she countered. All she could do was repeat that denial. Soon she started to wonder if maybe her husband was accusing her because he had something himself to feel guilty about, and she started venting her suspicions about him, and they ended up having a huge fight.

Neither one backed down, her husband finally announcing that if he found out it wasn't his child he'd divorce her. I don't know if you can do something like that when you're only three months along, but the next day the two of them trooped off to the hospital and insisted on getting a DNA test.

The nurse there explained how to calculate the due date and they realized they'd made a huge mistake. The baby had been conceived the night the husband had come back from a two-month business trip, their first night back together, when they'd made passionate love after his long absence. So they'd gotten worked up over nothing. Come to think of it, Yamagata works at the Adachi Manufacturing plant. Not that that matters... But it's good to be like those two, getting everything out in the open. Their doubts about each other were erased in one day. It would be awful for a woman, just because of problems figuring out a due date, to know her husband had doubts festering forever in his heart about an infidelity that never, ever happened.

There are other people who are the opposite, who breathe a sigh of relief when they miscalculate.

Like my brother-in-law—my older sister's husband.

Subtract *ten months and ten days* from August fourteenth and you get November fourth. He and I slept together on November twenty-first, so he figured it's not his child. That's what he thought, or rather what he convinced himself of.

And I never told him the baby is his. I told my parents and

sister that I couldn't reveal who the man was, that I'd had an affair with one of my bosses at work, and they believed it, my brother-in-law told me.

The child in my womb is, 100 percent, my brother-in-law's. But I can't blame him, since I was the one who seduced him. My sister first brought him to our house four years ago, and I've been in love with him ever since.

What do I love about him? More than looks or personality, it's his workplace…his profession, I mean. I came to love him because he's a police officer. I always enjoyed detective dramas on TV, but my special feelings for the police started on the day Emily was murdered.

You must have heard this from the other three girls, but right after the murder Maki told me to go to the local police station. It was on the way to school and I passed by there every day, but this was the first time I'd ever stepped inside. I'd never lost anything, or ever done anything particularly bad, so there was no reason to.

Though Emily did treat me as a thief. You didn't know that?

I'm sorry, but could we take a five-minute break? My stomach's killing me.

I think Maki spoke about the way we played Explorers, but wasn't it amazing that everything she said at that PTA meeting was out on the Internet? Apparently a parent was recording it all, which made me wonder—are you maybe recording this now? Not that it really matters…

I was the one who discovered that we could get into that abandoned cottage. Our family grows grapes, and the thing I hated most in the world was helping out with the farmwork. I thought it was totally unfair—that just because I was born into a farm family, I had to, for free, do the kind of labor I would never have had to do if I'd been born into an ordinary white-collar family. Not that I hated everything about it. Because of the cottage. The back of our fields faced the cottage grounds and whenever I was roped into helping out in the fields I'd take a break sometimes and wander around the grounds of the cottage as if I owned the place. The outside of the cottage was quite sophisticated and I tried many times to get a peek inside, figuring it, too, had to be gorgeous, but the windows and doors were boarded up tight.

If you took a snack or lunch and ate it underneath the large white birch next to the cottage, wouldn't you feel as if you were a girl from a foreign land having a tea party? It was my sister who came up with this idea. My sister, three years older than me, was good at thinking of ways to have a good time. I really loved my sister back then.

"We should take food that suits that cottage," my sister said, and she baked cookies and made some fancy sandwiches the night before we went to work in the fields. I say fancy, but they were actually quite ordinary. Supermarkets in the sticks don't sell any kinds of unusual hams or cheeses, so the sandwiches just had boiled eggs, roasted ham, cucumbers, and the like....But she wrapped them up like candy in cute wrapping paper, and made them heart-shaped. Then she placed them in a hamper lined with a strawberry-print handkerchief.

What with her bad asthma my sister seldom was asked to help out in the fields, so she made all this just for me. That's right, asthma. People who get it get it, even if they live in the town with the cleanest air in Japan.

One day at the beginning of June, during a break from farmwork, I headed to the cottage with some cookies she'd baked. The fields face the rear of the cottage, but on this day I noticed that something was a little different. The rear door, usually covered with a large board nailed over it, was now exposed. It was dark brown, with a gold-colored doorknob.

Maybe it's open, I thought excitedly, and turned the knob, but it was locked. Disappointed, I looked at the keyhole-shaped hole below the knob and remembered a TV drama where someone used a hairpin to unlock a door. I took the hairpin I'd used to pin back my bangs and inserted it into the keyhole. I wasn't expecting it to work but enjoyed how excited it made me feel. I moved the pin around inside the keyhole, felt it snag on something, then slowly turned it and heard a click as the lock opened. It didn't even take a minute.

I slowly pushed open the heavy door and inside was the kitchen. There were a few built-in shelves, but no plates or pots and pans. In back was a bar counter, and I felt as if I'd suddenly wandered into a house in a foreign land.

I wasn't brave enough to actually go inside. *I'll tell my sister about it* was my first thought, but I hesitated to bring her to such a dusty place. When her symptoms got worse it was a real pain. So instead, the next day I told Maki about it. Maki always had great ideas about how to have fun—not as many good ideas as my sister, though.

Sometimes when we played there were lots of kids with us, but we'd get in trouble if the older kids at school or parents found out we'd snuck into the cottage, so we decided to keep the number low and invite only our classmates from the West District of town. The same girls who were there on the day of the murder.

As soon as I unlocked the door and the five of us, with bated breath, slipped inside, each of us started to frolic around the place. It was the first time I'd ever laid eyes on a real fireplace, a canopied bed, and a claw-footed bathtub. There were lots of things at Emily's house, too, I'd never seen before then, but nothing feels as empty as wonderful things you know belong to someone else. That cottage wasn't mine, of course, but it also didn't belong to any of the five of us. And besides that, even Emily was amazed, never having seen a fireplace before. The cottage was our shared castle, our secret hideout.

Emily had an interesting proposal now that we had this secret hideout. "Let's hide treasures inside the fireplace," she said. "Not simply treasures, but make them keepsakes of someone, and write a letter addressed to that person with each treasure we hide." We were the age when it's easy to make up things, and we got totally engrossed in this game, brought our treasures and stationery from home, and plunked down in the living room to write our letters. I addressed mine to my sister, who, I pretended, had died.

Dear sister, thank you for always being so kind to me. I'll do my best so Mom and Dad won't get too sad, so please have a good long rest in heaven.

That's what I wrote, as I recall. As I wrote it, it really did feel as if my sister had died, and I teared up a little. I put the letter, along with a pressed-flower bookmark she'd bought me on a school trip, into a pretty tin that Emily brought from home that she said had originally had cookies in it.

Each of us sealed our letter without showing it to the others, but we did show our treasures to each other. Sae put in a handkerchief, Maki a mechanical pencil, Akiko a key holder. Typical kidlike items. But Emily's was different. Her treasure was a silver ring with a red stone in it. Even country kids like us could tell it wasn't a toy. By then we should have been used to all the expensive things Emily owned, but that ring really captivated us.

"Can I try it on?" I asked casually, holding out my hand, but Emily said, "No one but me is ever allowed to wear this ring." It sounded like something a princess in a fairy tale would say. She carefully put it away in its case.

"Well then, you shouldn't have brought it," I muttered, half annoyed, as Emily was bent over hiding the cookie tin with all our treasures inside the fireplace. She seemed to have heard me.

It was a week after this that Emily came to my house.

It was Sunday afternoon and it had been raining since morning and I was lying around my room reading comic books, bemoaning the fact that we weren't going to be playing in the cottage today, when Emily appeared. We weren't particularly close so I was surprised that she would visit me by herself. I went to the front door and Emily said in a low but agitated voice, "Mama's looking for the ring. Yuka, help me go get it from the cottage."

She meant her treasure. "Did you take it without asking your mother?" I asked.

"It was in my mother's closet, but it's my ring," she said. I found that hard to grasp. In our house my mother often said she'd give us rings when we got bigger—her own engagement ring to my sister and a ring she got from Grandmother to me. Probably Emily meant something like that.

I soon understood why she'd come to see me. I was the only one who could use a hairpin to unlock the cottage door. When the other kids saw me take out the hairpin from my bangs and unlock the door, they all said they wanted to try it, and they each took turns. But for some reason no one else could manage it. Their hairpins were the same. You just had to snag it onto the hollow at the back of the hole and turn it, but no matter how much I explained it to them no one could find that spot. I didn't expect Akiko to, but Maki and Emily never had any trouble solving any problems at school and I was surprised they couldn't get it.

"Yuka, you're really clever," Sae told me then.

I was always so-so when it came to most things and I'd never thought of myself as clever, though I was always pretty good with my hands. I didn't have a strong grip but was able to open bottle tops that were on really tight, could untie rope that had gotten all knotted, and was always good at putting together the little do-it-yourself projects that came with manga magazines.

Emily and I headed to the cottage, were able to open the rear door with no problem, and went to the living room, where the fireplace was. "Thank you, Yuka. Just wait a second," Emily said, and stuck her face inside the fireplace. After a moment she turned around. "It's gone," she said.

We'd set the cookie tin in the right-hand corner in front, but when I looked in I couldn't find it. "You're right. It's gone," I said. I looked out from the fireplace to find Emily glaring at me.

"It's you, Yuka, isn't it!"

At first I couldn't figure out what she meant. Seeing Emily's cold eyes, though, I understood she was accusing me. I couldn't understand why, and I insisted, loudly, "It wasn't me!"

But Emily yelled right back. "It had to be you, Yuka! You're the only one who can unlock the door. You were angry I didn't let you wear the ring, that's why you took it. That's stealing. And I know you've stolen other things. You stole Sae's eraser. I saw you secretly using the eraser she thought she lost. If you don't give me back the ring I'm going to tell Papa."

Emily started crying loudly. "Give me back the ring. You thief—you thief…" There were a lot of things I felt like saying to her, but I figured none of them would do any good.

What kinds of things? The eraser that Sae lost was the same kind that all the girls from the West District had. At a Christmas party for kids the year before we'd all gotten them as presents. After Emily heard that Sae had lost her eraser she just happened to see me using an identical one, that's all. And I wasn't using it *in secret* or anything.

Now I wonder if Emily would have had the same thoughts about Maki or Akiko if one of them had been using the eraser.

What sort of eyes are *covetous* eyes, do you think? My mother has often told me, since I was a child, that that's the kind of eyes I have. My sister and I have the same single-lidded type of eyes, but I was the only one she said that to.

We were walking down the street once, my mother and I, and we passed a classmate with an ice cream cone. I just waved at my classmate the way you'd expect, but my mother scolded me. "Stop staring at what other people have," she said. "That's acting very greedy." She seemed disgusted. I mean, it was a hot day and I did think it would be nice to have some ice cream myself. But it wasn't as if I were dying to get some.

If you feel that way, I thought, *you should have given me better vision.* When I was in third and fourth grade my vision got really bad, and the glasses I wore didn't really correct it well, so I was always squinting at things. So that must be why she thought that.

Sorry, I've gotten sidetracked. I was talking about Emily's accusation.

Emily wouldn't stop crying and it made me upset, so I said, "I've had enough," left the cottage, and went home.

It was the evening of the same day that Emily came to our house along with her father. My mother showed them in. I was so worried they'd accused me of stealing that I hid out in the bathroom, but then my mother called to me in a very gentle voice to coax me out.

I went into the living room and my eyes met that goggle-eyed alien. Your husband. That's what kids in town used to secretly call him. You're laughing, but they used to call you that, too. . . . I'm sorry, let me continue.

The two of them were there to give me back my treasure, they said. When Emily was left behind at the cottage she didn't know what to do, because she couldn't lock it up by herself. She couldn't tell her mother about it since then she'd know that Emily had taken the ring and would be angry at her, so she used a pay phone near the cottage to call Adachi Manufacturing and ask her father to come help her. He was at work even though it was his day off.

Her father hurried right over from work and, as they stood in front of the cottage, Emily was telling him the whole story when a real estate agent from the next town over drove up. The real estate agent had earlier brought a client from Tokyo who wanted to start a free school here to see the cottage, and after he showed it to him in the morning the man had another appointment elsewhere in the afternoon, so the agent drove him to the station and was stopping by here one more time afterward. He was going to put in a more secure lock on the rear door to keep out intruders.

The client had apparently found the tin with our treasures. "You shouldn't go in like that anymore," the real estate agent said, and gave her back the tin. Emily held out my bookmark that had been in the tin, as well as a large box of sweets from a well-known store in Tokyo, and said, "These are really good, I hope you enjoy them." She was smiling at me but she didn't apologize for treating me like a thief. She thought she was the one who suffered the most, and that people would forgive whatever she said—that over time they would completely forget it. She was just like you.

I never told anybody about this, because I figured that the sweets she gave me were a bribe to keep my mouth shut about being treated as a thief. At first I refused to take them. "No thanks, I don't need those," I told her. The sweets were wrapped up beautifully, and I really did want to try them, but I planned to refuse until Emily apologized. But my mother butted in and accepted them.

"Emily and her father have come out of their way to see us, so you shouldn't act like that," my mother scolded me. "I'm sorry she's so unfriendly," she said, bowing her head. "I hope you'll still be friends." Emily and her father went home satisfied, but I was left feeling it was all so unfair. And Mother scolded me even more after they left.

Not because the fact that we'd snuck into the cottage came to light because of Emily. It was because my sister said, "I wanted to go into that cottage too. Why didn't you tell me about it?" And I said, "I figured it was too dusty." "Well, sorry I have asthma!" she said sarcastically, and then burst out crying.

"Why do you have to act so proud in front of your sister?" my mother said, upset with me, but I wasn't acting proud at all. After Emily and her father had left, my sister had come downstairs, wondering what was going on, and my mother had told her, "Yuka and those girls snuck into an abandoned house behind our field."

I was about to defend myself, but my sister got the first word in.

"It's not Yuka's fault," she said. "I should have been more patient."

Hearing this, Mother said, "It's not your fault, Mayu," and she let my sister choose first from the sweets Emily had brought.

My mother had always felt really bad about Mayu being born so sickly, and apparently felt bad, too, about never having given my father a son. But having given birth to a nearsighted girl like me? That never seemed to faze her.

Nearsightedness is from my father's side of the family, but neither my sister's condition nor Father's was Mother's fault. I never heard either of them blame her. I think she just liked to blame herself. Masochism, maybe? Something like that.

Still, don't you think it's awful that when her daughter got caught up in a murder she didn't run right over to her to be with her? ...

We've finally worked our way back to the murder.

But before I go on, could you wait another five minutes?

After Akiko and I split up that day at the rear entrance to the school, I ran straight to the police station. The policeman in charge of the small substation changed every two or three years, but at this time it was a young man named Mr. Ando, a huge slab of a man who would look good in a judo *gi*. I'd been ordered to tell him about the murder, but I was scared, afraid he might get mad about a child like me coming inside alone. Mr. Ando was talking with an old lady who'd come in to tell him something, and when I saw how kind he was to her I breathed a sigh of relief.

I'd come to report a murder and I had to tell him right away, so I should have interrupted them, but it was my first time in a police station, and I studiously stood off in a corner, waiting my turn as if I were in a hospital waiting room. Mr. Ando must have thought I didn't have anything very important to tell him.

In a gentle voice not at all in keeping with his appearance he said, "Please take a seat over here," motioning to me to sit in a folding chair next to the old lady.

The old lady was talking about the theft of the French dolls. The person who stole them had to be from Tokyo, she was saying in an older dialect that only old folks used, and I was hoping she'd finish soon. I suddenly remembered who she was, and recalled that the grandchild in her house had been bragging how she was going to Disneyland with her family over the Obon holiday. *The old lady must feel lonely with everyone gone*, I thought, and I felt a little sorry for her.

This was right after Emily was killed, of course. Are you disappointed I didn't feel scared because of the murder like the other kids? Truthfully I didn't feel scared yet. It wasn't that I was unfeeling or anything, or because Emily had accused me of being a thief. It was simply because I hadn't gotten a good look at what had happened.

Two days before the murder I had been cleaning house before our relatives came to visit and had stepped on the glasses I normally wore. So I was wearing an older pair of glasses and couldn't see very well.

So all I could make out in the dim changing room was that Emily was lying on the floor, and that wasn't enough to terrify me. It was only after I went back to the pool that I realized that something terrible had taken place.

The old lady left and the policeman turned to me. "Sorry to keep you waiting," he said kindly. "So, what's the matter?"

"My friend collapsed at the school pool," I said, describing to him what I'd seen.

"You should have told me that right away," the policeman said, and made a call for an ambulance. He may have thought it was a drowning. Right after that, he put me in his patrol car and we headed to the school.

The policeman finally understood that something alarming had happened when we arrived at the pool and he saw you. You were sitting there in the boys' changing room, holding Emily to you, calling her name out over and over. When I saw this it hit me, too, that Emily was actually dead.

It was probably better, in order to preserve the crime scene, not to hold the body like that, something the policeman gently hinted at, but I doubt his voice got through to you.

There was one more person there, Sae, but she was crouched down outside the changing room, eyes shut, hands held tight over her ears, and she didn't respond when we called her. So it was up to me to explain what had led up to this.

We were playing volleyball in the shade by the gym when a man in work clothes came over and asked if one of us would help him check the ventilation in the pool changing rooms. He took Emily off with him. We went on playing for a while but when the six o'clock music, "Greensleeves," started playing and she hadn't come back we went to check on her. That's when we found her lying in the boys' changing room.

The policeman listened intently, taking notes in a pocket notebook.

The ambulance arrived soon after, and a patrol car from the prefectural police, and people in the neighborhood started coming to see what was going on.... The area around the pool was soon swarming with people. Sae's mother ran up in a panic and carried her home on her back. Right after, Akiko's and Maki's mothers came, and I remember Akiko's mother being really upset, saying, "My daughter came home bleeding from her head." Maki's mother loudly called out her name, looking for her. But things were in such an uproar neither one of these mothers stood out from the crowd.

In the midst of all this I was left all alone. I was one of the people directly involved in the murder, yet no one paid any attention to me. The local policeman reported to the prefectural police who'd arrived what I'd told him.

Maybe the murderer is among the crowd here, I thought, *and might take me away without anyone realizing it.* There were so many people milling about, yet no one would rescue me.... Could anything be more frightening?

Wanting the policeman to pay attention to me, I tried my hardest to think if there was anything else I could report. I retrieved the volleyball from in front of the gym and handed it to him, telling him there might be fingerprints on it, and reenacted in the girls' changing room next door how Emily had been lying on the ground. I was desperate to be noticed.

As I was doing all this, the prefectural police came over to me and asked a lot of questions about the murderer. I was overjoyed that someone finally noticed me, and tried my best to recall, though the details, especially about the man's facial features, totally escaped me. It was less that I couldn't recall than that, as I said earlier, with my bad vision I hadn't seen much to begin with. As we tried to reach one hundred passes in a row, I was the one who blew it and sent the ball flying toward where the murderer stood. If I'd been wearing my usual glasses I would have seen his face better—maybe not down to little moles or scars or anything, but at least the main outlines of his features. But I hadn't and it frustrated me no end.

I was angry at my mother—the one who always told me to stand up on a chair and wipe down the dirty shelves because it was too dusty for my sister to do. And angry that, while half the town seemed to have gathered at the school grounds, my mother still hadn't shown up. Our house was in the West District but was pretty far from the school, and maybe she'd only just found out about this terrible event. *She should be here any minute now,* I thought, and was waiting for her. I was upset at her, but I still loved her a lot.

The investigation went on until late at night, but around 9 p.m. the policeman took me home. When I opened the door and my mother saw the policeman she looked sheepish.

"Oh, I'm so sorry you had to go to all this trouble," she said. "I was just about to go get her. Mrs. Shinohara phoned me that something terrible had happened at the school, but the thing is, my older girl hasn't been feeling well since this morning. Yes, she has very bad asthma. She couldn't eat a bite, but in the evening she said she might take a bit of vegetable soup, and I was just preparing it for her. It's my special cold potage that she manages to get down no matter how poorly she's feeling. And my husband is the eldest son, so as you can see we're pretty busy with relatives on Obon...."

A person had just been murdered, yet Mother could smile and carry on like this. I started to cry. I'm not sure if it was because I felt miserable, or sad.... I remembered you, sobbing loudly as you held your dead daughter. If my sister had been killed I'm sure my mother would sob like that too, but if it was me who was murdered she probably wouldn't even show up.

My father? He'd been drinking with male relatives all afternoon and by evening had basically passed out. If he had been up, I doubt whether he would have come to get me either. "Too much trouble," I can imagine him saying. He was the heir in the family and had been excessively indulged growing up, but when it came to any child who wasn't going to be his heir, especially his disappointing younger daughter, it seemed as if he couldn't care less. Not that he had a ton of money to pass on—he certainly didn't.

As I kept on crying, Mother hit me with an additional verbal blow.

"You're in fourth grade," she said. "You should have come home on your own."

Then I wouldn't have been so embarrassed, I heard a voice inside me add. It didn't matter to them if I was alive or not. And if my parents were like this, it was like my own blurry view of the world—nobody else was about to notice me either, no matter how good their vision.

As I was thinking all this, the policeman beside me said to my mother: "I'm the one who kept her from coming back. Please accept my apology."

He turned to me, bent his huge frame over, and gave me a pat on the head.

"You must have been scared," he added. "So thank you for telling me all about it. Let us policemen handle everything else now. You go and rest up."

His large, rugged, warm hand nearly enveloped my whole head. I never forgot what it felt like. And ever since that day I've been searching for a hand that would make me feel that way.

The biggest change after the murder was my sister's attitude toward me.

My mother, perhaps feeling bad that she was the only mother who hadn't gone to get her daughter, started being unusually kind to me. "Are you hungry?" she asked. "Is there anything special you'd like to eat? Shall I go to the video shop in the next town and get a fun video for you?" That's about the size of it, but it was a first, her being this solicitous.

"Okay, then I'd like gratin," I told her.

But that night on the dinner table were cold noodles, steamed chicken, and a shredded dried plum salad. "Your sister can't eat hot things," Mother explained, "they make her asthma act up." And as to the video, my sister hated noisy anime, so in the end Mother didn't rent one for me.

So it was all about my sister. I mean, everybody figured it would have been better if the one who'd been killed was me.

Unable to stand it anymore, I knocked over the bowl of noodles and screamed. I'd never acted like that before. I'd always thought my sister had it bad and I tried to be patient. But now it was clearly me who was having a hard time. And that set off my sister, who burst into tears.

"I'm so sorry," she said. "It's all my fault. If only I were healthier Yuka wouldn't have to feel this way. And I could have made gratin for Yuka myself, since she's feeling so down.

I wish I hadn't been born like this, with this body.... Why do I have to be the one who suffers like this? *Why*, Mom? *Tell me....*"

As she tearfully complained to Mother, Mother said, "I'm so sorry, Mayu. Forgive me," and held my sister to her tight and burst out crying loudly. This was the day after the murder.

After that, whenever I had to go with my mother to be interviewed by the police, my sister's symptoms would act up and Maki's mother would take me instead. News about Emily's murder was on TV, and when my father asked me what the police had questioned me about, my sister would say it was all so awful she'd lost her appetite, and lay down her chopsticks. Gradually the murder became a taboo topic since it upset Mayu. Just as before, she was the one everyone worried about, and I was basically a nonentity.

I knew complaining about it was pointless, but that didn't mean it didn't affect me. Far from it. I grew more anxious by the day. I was sure the police would soon catch the murderer, but there was no sign of any impending arrest. Which may have been, in a sense, because of us. We were just children, but still there were four of us witnesses and yet all four said we couldn't remember the man's face. I could understand how Sae, basically a coward, and Akiko, who was always kind of spacey and now had a head injury, might not recall. But I couldn't believe that Maki, too, wouldn't remember. I mean, even *I* could remember everything I'd been able to see.

But I don't think that was the sole reason the investigation hit a snag. The day of the murder had been Obon. If the murderer had come to town by car, normally someone would have noticed an unfamiliar vehicle. But during Obon families came in droves, more of them in cars than by train, the town filled with out-of-town license plates and rental cars, so I bet there weren't many reports of suspicious cars.

Plus, even if people saw someone they didn't recognize walking in town, unless they were blood-spattered or something they'd just think it had to be somebody's relative visiting. So even if the murderer had changed out of his work clothes and stuffed them into a Boston bag, people would only put him down as an out-of-town relative visiting for the holidays.

Until the year before, people might have wondered who a stranger was if they happened to run across him on the street, even during Obon. But after the Adachi Manufacturing plant was built, the town was crawling with people we didn't know, so I think fewer people paid attention to strangers. Sort of like the indifference of city folk.

Maybe being indifferent feels good once you're used to it, but I was yearning for the opposite: someone to pay attention to me. What came to mind then was the policeman who took me home the night of the murder, Mr. Ando. I knew if anyone would, *he* would listen to everything I had to say, and protect me from the murderer. I began to desperately think of excuses to visit the police substation.

Someone like you, who's friendly and sociable, might wonder why I had to have a reason to visit. You would just stroll in, say hello with a smile, and chat about school or other topics. But that was beyond me. If I'd taken a step inside and he'd asked, "What's the matter?" and I'd been unable to answer, I think I would have run out the door. Apart from the way they treated my sister, since we were a farming family, ever since I can remember, even on Saturdays I was told, "We're busy, don't bother us." There was no one to teach me that I didn't need a special reason to want to act a little spoiled sometimes, to want to have people pay attention to me.

At first I visited the police station to report on things I thought might be clues in the murder. For instance, though I couldn't remember the murderer's face, his voice reminded me of that of a certain actor. And the fact that though there were twenty-some homes in the West District that had French dolls, the ones that were stolen were all from our ten best list. Not the kind of information that would be very helpful, and in less than five visits I'd run out of material.

I went to the police station, too, when I found coins dropped along the road. But that didn't happen so often, so I started using hundred-yen coins from my own purse. Now that I think of it, it's like one of those host bars, paying for a man to be with you and talk with you. And actually about ten years after this I was really into that kind of bar for a while. It's only now, really, that I realize why I wanted to go to those places.

You know, I truly hate you, and I can't say I'm enjoying this, but when I talk with someone I begin to realize things I wouldn't on my own. After the murder the four of us didn't play together again and never once talked together about the murder. But maybe if we *had* talked more all these awful things wouldn't have happened.

Awful things in my case means...It was six months after the murder when I shoplifted for the first time.

Oh, it hurts.... Please give me another five minutes.

I ended up estranged from the girls I'd played with every day, and my sister, always so kind to me, now treated me as an enemy. I was convinced all over again that my parents didn't love me, and eventually I ran out of reasons to visit the police station. I was truly, truly lonely....

One day I needed a special 4B pencil for school, for drawing class, but all I had in my purse was ¥30. "I need a pencil for drawing class," I told my mother, and she said, "I just gave you your allowance. Use that." I didn't tell her the truth and went to the stationery store, only to find that the pencil cost ¥50.

The stationery store was a small shop near school, run by an older lady. The pencils were in an upright plastic cylinder display, and I took one out and thought, *What should I do? What should I do?* clutching the pencil tightly.... And I slipped it into the sleeve of my jacket. I couldn't believe what I'd done and turned away toward the door to hide from the shopkeeper. I nearly screamed. There beyond the glass door stood my sister, facing me.

When she stepped inside she said, "You came to buy a 4B pencil, right? I have one, so you could have used that. Did you already buy one?"

Silently I shook my head.

"Good. I came to buy a mechanical pencil. Why don't I buy one for you, too? I doubt any other kids at elementary school have one. You can brag about it. Let's get the same kind, but in different colors. Which would you like, pink or light blue?"

My sister smiled and held out two cute mechanical pencils to me, each one costing ¥300. This was the first time she'd smiled at me since the murder and it puzzled me, so I just stared silently at the pencils. Why was she being so nice to me today? Did something good happen to her? Hesitantly I was reaching out for the light blue pencil when I felt something hard jab against my arm. The pencil inside my sleeve.

Maybe she'd seen me steal it and planned to tell Mother about it when she got home. If my shoplifting came out they'd fawn over her even more, and act even more disgusted with me. My sister could hardly wait for that. Should I take out the pencil from my sleeve, tell her I didn't need the mechanical pencil, and ask her to buy this one instead? But I had no idea what she would say if I took the stolen pencil out.

As I agonized over this, my sister was browsing through the selection of erasers and colored ballpoint pens, and unable to stand the guilt—or rather the feeling of despair—of my sister having caught me red-handed shoplifting, I ran right out of the shop. I didn't go home, and having no friends I could visit, before I realized it I was heading toward the police station. It's a little strange to go to a police station right after shoplifting, but I understood that was the only place that would take me in.

I got to the police station but did hesitate about going inside. Mr. Ando, though, spotted me and called me to come in.

"Hello there, Yuka! Sure is cold today, isn't it. Come inside and warm up."

It wasn't *Why did you come here? What's wrong? Did some-*

thing happen? Just *Sure is cold.* I took the pencil out of my sleeve. "I stole this," I said, "I'm so sorry," and burst out crying. I didn't do that in order to be forgiven or anything. He could have gotten angry, that was okay with me. In fact, that's what I wanted.

But Mr. Ando wasn't angry. He sat me down in the chair next to the kerosene stove and took out a clear plastic bag from his desk drawer. Inside were close to thirty ¥100 coins.

"These aren't coins people actually lost, are they," he said. "I think you were concerned about how the investigation was going and brought them here, pretending someone had dropped them. I'm sorry we haven't been able to find the murderer. I know that's made you scared. You don't need to do something like that—you can come here anytime you like. You don't need a special reason. Now, take this and go pay for what you took. Tell the shopkeeper you forgot your purse and went to get it and she'll forgive you."

Mr. Ando put the bag of coins into my hands. His large hand covering mine and the bag felt as reassuring as it did the day of the murder. It made me feel I wasn't alone. I thanked Mr. Ando and went to the stationery shop, but the lady who ran it told me my sister had paid for me. The lady hadn't noticed I had shoplifted, and my sister had told her everything and apologized for me. "What a wonderful sister you have," the lady said.

When I got home my mother met me at the door and wouldn't let me in. Instead, she locked me inside the shed. "Children who steal stay inside here until morning," she said. There was no light there, or bedding, but when I took out the coins from the plastic bag and recalled the feeling of the policeman's hand, I wasn't frightened or sad at all.

What did make me sad was Mr. Ando leaving the following month. He'd passed his exams and was being reassigned to the prefectural police headquarters, a promotion for him but a terrible blow for me. On the day he was to leave I was standing there mute, head hung, outside the police station, unable to think of a nice way to say goodbye. When he saw me Mr. Ando said, "A veteran policeman will be taking my place, so come see him anytime if anything is worrying you." The man who took his place, though, an older, stooped-over man with a family of his own, didn't look very reliable, so I never visited the police station again.

And that's why—and this might sound self-serving, I know—I frequently shoplifted after that. I didn't do it because it was fun, or because I didn't have enough spending money. I just wanted somebody to pay attention to me. They hadn't come to get me when there was a murder, but I figured if the police called my parents to come to the station to get me, they'd have to. But maybe my dexterity worked against me, for hardly any of the shop owners ever noticed I was shoplifting. The only ones who did notice, and talk to me, were a group of junior high school kids who hung around town till late at night. Finally I had a group to be with.

This was a year after the murder. It was two years after that when you called us all to your home.

Three years after the murder you called the four of us, now thirteen years old, to your place and told us something unbelievable. Girls that age, even if they're living completely ordinary lives, are full of doubt and anxieties about their identity, but you called us all *murderers*. And told us we must either find the man who murdered Emily or else perform an act of penance that would satisfy you. Otherwise, you'd get revenge.

Did you ever really consider what effect this passing emotional outburst of yours would have on children? After you moved back to Tokyo, didn't you completely forget all about it in a couple of days?

You and Emily might not have looked much alike, outwardly, but your personalities were very much alike. And... your personalities were very much like my own sister, too.

My sister went back to acting like the kind older sister she'd always been about two months before you called me to your house. The reason was pathetically simple. She was in high school now and had a boyfriend, a guy who treated her like a princess. They saw each other every day in school, yet still talked on the phone till late at night, and on days when we didn't have school, she'd stay out late with him. She showed me photos they'd taken with a disposable camera, excitedly telling me how they'd ridden the roller coaster at an amusement park five times in a row. I had no idea how to react.

Mom was happy, saying, "Now that she's growing up she'll get stronger physically," but still she worried about my sister. "Wasn't going out too much for you?" she'd ask. "What did you have for lunch? Maybe it'd be better next week if you stay at home and not go out?"

Once my sister had a boyfriend, these kinds of remarks, so much a part of our daily conversation, became distasteful to her. I always thought she was the type to be fawned over, but it turned out she was more the type who liked to monopolize someone else.

With my sister finding her concern so disagreeable now, Mother started meddling in my life. I thought it a little self-centered of her, though I can't say it bothered me that much. "Maybe you should see a doctor for psychosomatic illnesses," my mother advised me one day, taking me by surprise. It had been three years since the murder, so why say that now? Also, I didn't see how the murder had had any particular repercussions in my daily life.

When I told Mother there was no need for that, she tearfully told me this: "I think your shoplifting and running around at all hours stems from that murder. I mean, you never did anything like that before. You're basically a serious child, so I was sure that over time you'd get over it, but the murderer hasn't been found and you're getting worse. I haven't said anything, and the store owners don't catch you at it very often, but I know you shoplifted again yesterday. That look in your eyes tells me. That's why I'm saying this."

I'd been sure nobody knew what I was up to. And Mother never seemed to care what I was doing, just what my sister was. So I never dreamed she was onto me. And saying she could tell from my eyes…what kind of eyes did she mean? I went back into my room, imagined I was going to shoplift, and studied my face in the mirror. But nothing looked any different.

I was already thinking of stopping shoplifting. And at that time you called me to your house. That's why after I came home from your place I promised my mother I'd never shoplift again. I blamed it on you threatening me that I had to *remember the murderer's face*. "That scared me," I told my mother, "and before I knew what I was doing I was shoplifting. But it's okay now," I said. "Because Emily's mother's moving back to Tokyo."

I cut my ties, too, with the kids I'd run around with at night and lived a quiet, serious life. I was younger than the others in the gang, so they didn't really care if I quit. I graduated from high school and was one of only two local people hired by a savings and loan in a nearby town, so I guess you could say I did my very best. Maybe this was because you weren't around anymore.

Don't look at me like that. I'm just stating the facts. What you did that day was nothing less than intimidation. Threatened by you, the other three girls chose penance. It was stupid for them to do that—they hadn't done anything wrong. I'd planned on ignoring it all, but in the end I decided to take the second option.

I would find the murderer.

I didn't do it for you, though.... I did it for my brother-in-law.

The contractions are coming quicker now, so let me speed things up here.

My older sister got married four years ago. She'd graduated from a junior college in a city in this prefecture and had worked in a department store for three years when she got married. After she married she quit the job. Six months before they got married my sister brought her fiancé to our house in town. I was living in an apartment in a nearby town and came back the day before to help Mother clean the whole house and welcome the two of them. This time I didn't break my glasses.

My sister's fiancé was tall and lanky, with a pale, friendly face, exactly the type to be working in a department store, I figured.... But my sister told us he was a policeman in the prefectural police department. Our whole family stared at him, the doubt showing on our faces, wondering if someone like him could actually capture bad guys. Almost apologetically, my future brother-in-law explained that he was with the information section of the police and spent all his time in front of a computer. This was the first time I'd heard the police had a section like that, but I could definitely picture him working with computers all day.

I asked where the two of them had met and they said it was at a mixer. A lady, a saleswoman for a life insurance company whose territory included both the department store and the police department, had set up the party. The perfect way for them to have met, I thought, since my sister was always good at getting a man she was interested in to notice her. So I was surprised to hear that it was her fiancé who had fallen in love at first sight and had pursued her. He sounded a bit moonstruck as he related the story.

Appearance-wise, her fiancé was the type my sister had always gone for, but he wasn't my type, so I simply greeted him, shook his hand, and wished them well. And that's when it happened. His hand felt exactly the same. The same as that policeman, Mr. Ando...

My memories don't rely much on the visual. It wasn't his looks so much as the feeling of his hand that made me realize *I want him.* I wanted to touch his hands, be touched by them, have them all to myself. Not that that wish was ever going to be fulfilled. On that day, and from then on, he only had eyes for my sister.

What I always wanted was what my sister had. Not that she ever maliciously snatched away things that were mine. From the time I was born, my mother was entirely hers, and my brother-in-law, too, from the time I met him. That's all I mean.

Two years ago my sister went through a terrible time. She had a miscarriage and wasn't able to have any children after that. It was the busy season for farmers, and my parents couldn't help her much, so she stayed at my apartment for a while to regain her strength. But when she heard that one of her former classmates had had a baby, she burst out sobbing, and did the same whenever there was a diaper commercial on TV. Two weeks later, though, she seemed over it, and light-heartedly went back to the police housing in the city she lived in with her husband.

She got a part-time job in her old department store and used her pay to take trips with the friends she had back when she was single. My brother-in-law? He was always so busy at work that it didn't seem to make any difference to him if she was home or not. He was happy just seeing that she was well again.

But my sister made a terrible mistake.

I've gone out with six men altogether.... Is it so surprising? Even someone like me can get a boyfriend, you know. None of the relationships lasted very long, though.... The men all said I was too needy. When all I wanted was just to make them happy.... Did the murder traumatize me, is that what you're asking? I'd have to definitely say no. That was probably because I didn't clearly see the way Emily's dead body was, the state of her clothing, and so on.

Anyway, all the men I went out with were big, as if they did judo or rugby, so my sister figured that's the type of man I like, and she was sure I wasn't interested in someone like my brother-in-law. She didn't notice at all that I *wanted* him, and she asked me to take care of the housework while she was gone.

No, maybe she did notice.... She was, after all, the one who'd first realized I was shoplifting, so she should have understood my feelings for her husband. She knew, yet believed my brother-in-law wouldn't betray her, and was perhaps enjoying seeing my reaction. If that's the case, then she brought it on herself.

I wanted to go there every day, but considering the time and distance I could only go on weekends to help with housework. I enjoyed it so much.... I'd go there on Saturday morning, prepare lunch, and then my brother-in-law and I would eat it, just the two of us. Sometimes we'd watch movies, play games.... In the evening when I told him I had to be going and headed toward the door, he never stopped me. Except for one time.

Last November, the news came out about an information breach in our prefectural police department. Was it widely reported throughout the country? I don't know. A top secret file containing the name, address, and background of a minor who'd committed a juvenile crime was inadvertently emailed to the entire mailing list on the town's anticrime network. That news.

That was my brother-in-law's fault. More accurately, it was due to a new type of computer virus some hacker had infiltrated their system with, but my brother-in-law was the IT person in charge so he was severely punished. My sister had made a reservation for a trip to a resort in Hokkaido and went ahead with it, saying it would be a shame to have to pay the cancellation fees, so my brother-in-law and I were alone at the time.

The hands I'd wanted for so very long were, for just one night, mine. This happened two weeks after August fourteenth minus 280 days. But that's not where it all ended. Because a new life began to grow inside me. This child struggling to be born right now...

Excuse me. I need a minute here....

When I learned I was pregnant, I felt I'd acquired some amazing thing I just had to have.

I could give birth to my brother-in-law's child, a child my sister would never be able to have. Maybe when the child was born he'd divorce her and marry me. That's what I was hoping for, and it felt as if it could really come true.

My parents were shocked, my mother complaining that she couldn't face our relatives and neighbors because of the shame of my having an affair and getting pregnant. But when my father said to her, "But this means we have an heir now," she started to be more upbeat about the situation, taking a pregnancy belly band, and me, to the local shrine to be blessed, and accompanying me to my doctor's appointments, though I insisted I'd be fine on my own. After we found out the baby was a boy, she was even kinder toward me, making all my favorite dishes whenever I came back home and letting me watch as much TV and as many videos as I liked. Even when my sister was with me.

My sister had started smoking after she began working again, and whenever she pulled out a cigarette my mother would reprimand her, which really touched me. Amazing, right? She treated me much better than after the trauma of the murder. Made me think how wonderful being pregnant can be.

Still, it was pretty boring. I had terrible morning sickness and had to quit my job, but once I got to the stable, post–morning sickness period, I felt great and regretted not having taken a leave of absence.

And I thought I should do something that would make my brother-in-law happy. I recalled my sister saying that during the next personnel reassignments he might be sent off to some prefectural backwater. The complacent thought struck me how nice it would be if he could man the little police substation in whatever town he ended up in, but then I realized how tough this demotion had to be for him. Something nice I could do for my brother-in-law, for my brother-in-law the policeman...

If he could do something really great, maybe he wouldn't have to leave the prefectural headquarters. Like, for instance, capturing a murderer...Emily's murder was soon going to reach the statute of limitations.

These thoughts ran through my head, but then I thought: *If it were that easy, the police would have long ago arrested the murderer.* Okay, then how about some new information on the case? That would be enough. I felt as if I'd received a divine revelation.

Have you heard the idea that pregnant women often win the lottery? I don't think that's just a superstition. You're nurturing this new life inside you, so it's not strange that you might possess a kind of divinely inspired power.... Looking back on it now, though, I see I was just being a bit oversensitive.

This happened in April of this year. The divine revelation came to me over the radio. Your eyes get easily tired, don't they, when you're pregnant? That's why I had the radio on that day. Do you recall the news from last summer about a boy living in some free school who set fire to the place?

They were going to reopen the school and there was an interview with the director. They asked about why free schools were necessary, and about increased juvenile crime, and I was just half listening when I realized my heart was suddenly pounding.

Why was my heart racing?...It was because of the man's voice. It was like that of the man who killed Emily. Still, though, unless there was something really special about a man's voice, perhaps they all sounded more or less the same.

The man's voice was crisp and easy to understand, but that's about all that distinguished it—otherwise it was perfectly ordinary. I'd had two or three teachers in high school and junior high who sounded similar. *Maybe it was just my desire to find the murderer that made his voice sound like this to me?* I thought, finding it funny.

But there was one other thing about this news report that

bothered me. *Free school:* there were a few kids like Akiko in our country town who were self-imposed shut-ins, but none of them were attending a *free school* or anything. Still, the word sounded familiar and I now remembered why. On the day Emily accused me of being a thief, she'd mentioned how a person had come wanting to convert the cottage into that kind of alternative school.

The cottage was never sold, though, and five years ago was torn down. The real estate agent showing the property back then had already left on that day, but I knew him because just before the end of the fiscal year he'd come by our house to try to get my parents to buy that land. It was within walking distance and, without any expectations, really, more like just killing time—actually feeling more as if I were searching for a new place to live for me, my brother-in-law, and our baby—I went to see the real estate agent at his office near the station.

When the agent saw my swollen belly he asked, a bit expectantly, "You're looking for a new place to live, I imagine?" But when I said I wanted to ask about the person who, fifteen years ago, had visited the cottage thinking to make it into a free school, the agent was clearly disappointed.

"As I recall," he said, "they told me a free school built in the countryside would mainly be for problem kids from the city, so it had to be in a place that was convenient to get to. But managing a place like that has to be hard. I mean, that other place was burned down and all. When I saw it on TV I was really surprised to see it was the same man from then."

This is what the agent told me. The man whose voice sounded like the murderer's actually visited the cottage two months before Emily was killed? *If that's true, that's an amazing discovery,* I thought. But having come this far, and confirming it as a fact, actually made it harder to believe. Okay, then what should I do? Tell my brother-in-law? I was terribly confused.

But if that was all I had to go on, then so what? Two months before the murder, a man whose voice, in my opinion, resembled that of the murderer visited that town. But a voice wasn't much proof of anything at all. Plus, there was the French doll theft to consider.

I needed some more decisive proof. Fingerprints or something... What did Emily say back then? Didn't she say that the one who found our treasures was the person who came to see the cottage? *I wonder if he touched my bookmark? Didn't they get any fingerprints from the volleyball?* After he took Emily away, we went on passing the ball, so it's doubtful there'd be any useful prints, but say they did discover some—and those prints matched the ones on my bookmark—this could really be something. I didn't have good memories of the bookmark, but I had kept it all these years as a kind of memento of Emily.

I have to tell my brother-in-law....

Right around this time something awful happened. My sister tried to commit suicide. I'd come back to visit my parents, and she was back too, and slit her wrists in the bathtub. The cuts were shallow and not life-threatening. I think it was more a demonstration than anything. Mother blamed herself, of course, for having given my sister such a weak constitution that she'd had a miscarriage, but that couldn't be the reason for the suicide attempt. I think my sister realized the baby I was carrying was her husband's.

My brother-in-law blamed himself and was with her every moment after that, taking care of her. Whether it was because of the troubles at his work, or because of the baby, I lost my chance to talk with him about the murder. And besides, it didn't seem to matter anymore. Giving birth to a child wasn't going to make him mine, and I no longer *wanted* him as much as I did before. I decided I would give birth to this new life growing inside me on my own, and raise the baby on my own. This baby would be the only one who would need me.

I think this *ten months and ten days* is a time period given to me to let me really feel I'm going to be a mother.

But it was you who wouldn't allow me this.

Oh, it hurts. Let me stop for a moment again....Don't touch me! I don't want you stroking my back!

I didn't want to think any more about the murder, but then I got a letter from you. A copy of the letter from Sae. And then I got a copy from the weekly magazine website where Maki's confession was uploaded, and your letter. I call it a letter, but it was only one line:

I've forgiven all of you.

Isn't this strange, though? What are you accusing us of doing to you, and to Emily? When you read the letter from Sae, didn't it occur to you that you had driven her to murder her husband? When you found how the words you spit out that time, over ten years ago, weighed down on this girl more than you could ever have imagined, you didn't know what to do, did you? Panicking, you made copies of the letter and sent them to the other three of us. Even so, one of the other girls then killed someone.

You sent the letter because you wanted us to stop obsessing over what you'd told us, and you regretted that this didn't get across, so this time you appended your own message. But still one of the other girls killed someone. That girl said she hadn't read the letter. You thought that at least you could save the final girl, which is why you've come directly to see me now.

You're acting ridiculous. You blame yourself that things have come to this, but at the same time you seem so full of yourself. Isn't that why you say you forgive us?

At Sae's wedding ceremony, if you'd just apologized to her, told her you were sorry you'd said those awful things to her, I wonder if she would have felt so fixated on the promise she made to you. If, along with Sae's letter, you had only added one more line to the effect that we should forget the promise we made back then, I doubt Maki would have felt as driven into a corner as she did. I don't know how much you affected Akiko, but what's happened with me has nothing to do with any of that.

But didn't you really come here much earlier?

I was really shocked to read in Maki's confession the name of the man who ran the free school. The thought crossed my mind that I should get in touch with her. I first thought about contacting her younger sister....And just then the incident with Akiko took place. The incidents involving Sae and Maki happened in faraway towns, so the gravity of their having killed someone didn't really hit me so much, but Akiko's took place in our hometown. I'm no policeman, so no one would have blamed me if I accused that man of being the murderer and it turned out he wasn't. I was less worried about that than about finally putting an end to it all.

I told my brother-in-law I had something really important to tell him and asked him to come to my apartment. How he interpreted *important* here was clear as soon as he arrived at my door. He threw himself down on his knees, bowed his head to the floor, and said, "I'll help out financially as much as I can, but please don't tell anyone that child is mine." My protruding belly kept me from seeing his face, but it was obvious how upset he was. Maybe before he left the house my sister had said something to him. My apartment was on the second floor next to the staircase. Anyone might pass by, yet he remained there, on his knees, head bowed pitifully, apologetically pleading with me not to let anyone know it was his child. The thought that a man like this was the child's father made me feel miserable. Why should I have to tell him the critical secret I had?

And then this thought struck me. If I went to the prefectural police, Mr. Ando might be there. Why hadn't I thought of that before?

Telling my brother-in-law wouldn't help, so I gave up the idea. I had left the apartment and started to walk away when he grabbed me and pinned me from behind. No expression of affection, that's for sure. "Never, ever tell Mayu about this," he hissed, mistakenly thinking I was on the way to see her. Still keeping me pinned, he forced me over to the staircase.

My brother-in-law was trying to kill me. No—not me, but the child in my womb. Even though it's his child, he was willing to kill what was precious to me for the sake of my sister, for *her*—and there was no way I was going to let that happen!

No matter how angry I was, though, no matter how desperate I was to protect my baby, my brother-in-law was, after all, a man, and a policeman, lanky and thin though he might be. I struggled hard but couldn't break free. He pushed me to the edge of the stairs. One of my feet slipped and I was sure I was going to fall. And right then the cell phone in the pocket of my jumper rang. The theme song for a famous detective drama. At that very instant my brother-in-law, startled, relaxed his grip.

I twisted away and with my one free hand pushed him in the chest as hard as I could.

I'm sorry. It's a text from my sister.

Seems like my brother-in-law didn't make it.

The phone call at that moment was from you. After my brother-in-law tumbled down the stairs, I pulled out my phone to call an ambulance, and there was a number not in my contacts listed on the incoming calls. It bothered me, but first I had to call the ambulance and, after it arrived, tell the EMTs what happened.

"It was my fault," I explained. "I'd remembered something that could be a clue to a murder fifteen years ago and had my brother-in-law, a policeman, come here so I could ask him about it. We were going to go together to the police station and were rushing out when I nearly slipped on the stairs.... My brother-in-law tried to keep me from falling and he slipped and fell. I am so, so sorry. So very sorry..."

As I stood there crying, my stomach began to hurt, and

though it's a little early I had them take me in the same ambulance to the hospital. So here I am. Soon after that you called me, said you were in the area and wanted to meet, so I had you come to the hospital. But I was wondering—had you come to the apartment first? And seen everything that took place? The timing of your phone call was a bit too good to be true.

...Ah, so I'm right.

You're happy you were able to help me? Or maybe you couldn't stand it, knowing that the last of us four also ended up killing someone, and right before your eyes?...You couldn't stand it? Then why didn't you call out to me sooner? Didn't you come to my apartment, see a man was visiting me, and out of curiosity wait and see how it would all play out?

In the end your apologetic feelings toward us weren't genuine. You might still hate us, thinking we were responsible for Emily's murder.

This is what I thought. That we just happened to be caught up in the murder. That the murderer didn't just choose Emily from the five of us, but had his eyes on Emily from the start. And that her treasure, that ring, had something to do with it, and that you, who owned the ring, were involved.

I think maybe you know the man who ran the free school, this Mr. Nanjo.

My proof is...the rumor I heard from that friend of mine—the one who argued with her husband over the due date of their baby—that Emily is not really your husband's child. They got a new president in your company not long ago, didn't they, and I understand all sorts of things happened. The rumor may be groundless. But I get the feeling it can't be totally dismissed. And I'm not just relying on a pregnant woman's intuition.

Emily's almond eyes, for one thing, don't resemble either yours or your husband's. Can we really ignore genetics? Another thing, when you called the four of us to your house, this is what you said: "I'm her parent, and I'm the only one who has that right."

The only one...

I don't know if it will prove anything, but I'm giving you the bookmark. To thank you, I hope, for saving this baby inside me.... I was sure that of the four of us I was the only one unaffected by the murder, but it turns out what you said to us held me in its grip as well.

All four of us have now kept our promise to you. And what do you plan to do with that? You definitely have money, and power. You can go ahead and tell the police that I pushed my brother-in-law. I don't mind. I'll leave this, too, up to you. But even if you don't tell, don't expect me to thank you for protecting me.

I think I'd better get over to the OB-GYN ward soon. It's been a long day. A long fifteen years. I'm just glad my precious treasure's birthday won't be the fourteenth of August.

That's all.

Penance

If it was my fault that all of you committed your crimes, then how should *I* do penance for that?

Ever since the day I moved to that town—a place that was far more inconvenient to live in than I had ever imagined— all I wanted was to go back to Tokyo. The material inconveniences were, of course, hard to put up with, but worse was how closed-minded the people were. They treated me as if I were some foreigner.

Just going out shopping for something I felt it—the eyes scanning me from top to bottom, people whispering, making fun of me. "Look at how dressed up she is. Maybe she's on her way to a wedding?" At the supermarket, every time I asked if they had a particular item they'd cluck their tongues and make a comment like "That's what these city types are like."

It's not as if I were asking for something so unusual. Beef shanks, Camembert cheese, canned demiglace sauce, fresh cream... Just asking for items like this made them treat me like some stuck-up rich lady.

Despite this, I did try to get closer to them. For my husband's sake. If he hadn't had such a high position I doubt I would have tried so hard to fit in, but when you're the head of the newly built factory you have a duty. I had to do my utmost to help make the townspeople accept the new Adachi Manufacturing plant.

You know about the neighborhood cleanup campaigns? I took part once. "The news circular that made the rounds of the neighborhood said it was voluntary," I told the other wives at the Adachi company housing, "but we should get involved in these kinds of town events." I tried to get as many as I could to participate. But when we got to the local community center where everyone was to gather, the local people's attitude was unbelievable.

"You ladies from the big city don't need to trouble yourselves with this kind of activity.... How did you plan to help, all dressed up like that?"

That's the kind of thing they told us. And we'd gone there in shirts and jeans we didn't mind getting dirty, ready to help clean out ditches or whatever. Not that the townspeople were wearing wartime *monpei* work clothes or anything. Many of them had on sweats, but there were a few younger people dressed like me. If I'd had on sweats I wouldn't have been surprised if they'd made the same kind of comments. When everyone set off to clean up the neighborhood we were told, "We can't get those delicate white hands all dirty, now can we?" and while the locals went off to cut weeds along the roadside and the riverbank we, the outsiders, were assigned to wash windows at the community center.

I wasn't the only one upset with the local people's attitude. The other company wives often exchanged complaints about it in the hallways of our housing complex. This gradually led to a feeling of solidarity among people who, in the old factory, hadn't associated much with each other. They started getting together regularly for tea parties and becoming better friends.

But I was hardly ever invited to these parties.

Whenever the cake shop I loved back in Tokyo had a new kind of cake, my mother would send me some, and I tried inviting some of the wives in company housing over to enjoy them. But it was never much fun, and afterward those ladies didn't invite me to their own parties. This bothered me, since I wanted to vent my own complaints about the town to someone and ask the other wives about how they were handling cram school and lessons for their children and the like. But then it occurred to me that it was only natural that they exclude me, since one thing they wanted to complain about was the company.

"Why on earth would they build a factory way out here? We've just built a house in Tokyo, for gosh sakes. And just gotten an introduction to an excellent cram school program." I didn't have to strain my ears to pick up on all their complaints.

So within the closed-off world of the town there was another insular world, and I was excluded from both.

It wasn't like that when I lived in Tokyo. I always had a lot of friends, and we'd chat on and on, enjoy going to favorite boutiques and restaurants and attending plays and concerts. No one was so worn out with housework that they'd talk about a special sale on eggs or anything. All my friends and I cared about was self-improvement.... The ones who let me feel that happy, that content, were those friends I shared the best part of my life with.

Through various channels I've heard what's happened with all of you from the murder down to the present, and though I can feel sorry, it's hard to fully sympathize or imagine your situation.

Why didn't these children dress up, or play with friends, or enjoy life? Put in your situation, I wonder what kind of life I would have led.

I had a friend I'd known since childhood. Perhaps because we attended a private school, I don't recall ever playing in the school grounds after school or on holidays. Instead, we played together at a nearby park. What if some strange man had appeared there, taken one of my friends away, and killed her? And if the murderer was never caught, would I have lived in fear for years afterward? If the murdered friend's mother cursed me, would that have constantly preyed on my mind?

I don't think I would have held on to it as long as you four did.

I lost a friend of mine too. There was a time when I really blamed myself for it, thinking it was my fault. But then I told myself, *I can't go on brooding over it forever. I've got to be happy.*

I decided to live my life with that kind of clear-cut attitude. I was twenty-two then, a little younger than you all are now.

I got to be friends with Akie when I had just started my sophomore year in college, in the spring. I was in the English department, in a finishing school type of women's college. Most of the students, including me, had come up through the affiliated school system, from elementary school straight into the college without having to worry about entrance exams, but Akie was in the group from outside who had had to pass exams to matriculate. She mentioned her hometown once, but it had no famous tourist sites or well-known industry, and I'd never heard of it before.

I was always out having a good time, only attending classes just before exams, but Akie never missed class, always front row center, busily taking notes. The first time I talked with her was just before a test when I asked to borrow her notebooks. She hardly knew who I was, but she was happy to lend them to me.

And the meticulous notes she took were amazing. It made me think that next year they should give up using those thick old textbooks and use her notebooks for class instead. I thought of buying her some cake in the school cafeteria to thank her, but felt that wasn't enough, so I gave her one of the two concert tickets I'd happened to receive.

One of my boyfriends had given me the tickets, but I hadn't promised to go with him, so I thought it was okay to give one to Akie.

Would a girl like her, who seemed so super-serious, really

enjoy a boy-band concert? I wondered, but it turned out, surprisingly, she was a big fan of pop-idol singers. "No way! I love that group," she told me. "Are you sure it's okay? I feel bad, all I did was lend you my notebook." She was so happy that she treated me to a cup of tea.

It seemed as though this was the first time she'd had cake in the cafeteria, and she was deeply touched. "I've never had such delicious cake," she told me.

Akie started to interest me.

On the day of the concert she was a bit more dressed up than usual, though her shoes and handbag were the same old worn-out ones she always had. I wasn't all that interested in pop-idol singers, so instead of watching them singing and prancing about the stage, my eyes were more drawn to Akie's feet as she leaped up and down for all she was worth. How could she wear such worn-out shoes and not care at all? If those were the only shoes I had, I'd never leave home. *What kind of shoes would go well with that outfit?* I mused. *Maybe those green short boots I saw the other day.*

That's it, I decided—*I'll take her out shopping.* She only hung out with other girls from the country, so I was sure she had no idea where any fashionable shops were. Also, I wanted to buy her some really good cake, since she'd enjoyed the second-rate cake in the school cafeteria so much. I knew a nice bakery I was sure she would love.

She happily accepted my invitation. At the shoe store I asked her, "How about these shoes?" and she replied, eyes sparkling, "They're wonderful!" She told me she wanted to send some nice stationery for her younger sister's birthday, so

I took her to a store I knew. "You have such good taste, Asako, so why don't you choose?" she said, and when we had cakes she couldn't have been more excited. "I've never, ever tasted anything like this!"

I introduced her to some of the boys I hung out with, too. They took her on drives, and out drinking. Akie couldn't drink much and was a bit hesitant at first, but the boys were all good-looking and good conversationalists, and gradually she opened up. "Your friends are all so nice, Asako," she told me, and I said, "And you're one of my precious friends too." She beamed.

I was enjoying myself immensely.

Up to this time I'd thought it was only natural that people did things for me, and I had never once thought about making others happy. Every time a boyfriend gave me a present I always wondered why they wanted to do that, since I never did much of anything for them in return. But now I understood that they simply enjoyed giving.

It was so satisfying to see Akie's happy look and hear her thank me. *I guess maybe after all I'm the type,* I thought, *who prefers doing things for others over having them do things for me.*

If I had met the four of you, now twenty-five, under different circumstances—for instance, if Emily had lived and introduced you as her friends—I probably would have enjoyed giving you advice and buying you presents.

Sae, you have such fair skin and distinct features, if you cut your hair shorter you wouldn't look so timid. How about letting your ears show and wearing some largish earrings? I found some wonderful ones the other day and went ahead and bought them, so I'll give them to you. Why don't you wear them on your next date?

Maki, you're tall, but you still shouldn't wear flats. And you're a teacher, but that doesn't mean you need to dress frumpily. I've got it—how about a scarf? You have a long neck so it should look good on you.

Akiko, you need to go out more. You like cute things, right? I know so many great shops I'd love to take you to, I don't know where to start. I wonder if we could see them all in one day. Oh, and a friend of mine opened a flower-arranging school. We should go there together.

Yuka, you have such beautiful hands it's a shame to let them go. Have you ever been to a nail salon? I'd love to give you a ring as a present, but I suspect you wouldn't be that happy to get it from me.

And while I'm saying all this, Emily interrupts. "Stop it, Mama. You always act like this when my friends are over. You're such a busybody. And we've had enough tea and cakes, so leave us alone for a while."

And she'd shoo me out of the room....

Come to think of it, you did all come over to my place once, other than when the murder occurred. Just that one time, but I remember it well. None of you could even use a cake fork well, and I was wondering whether it was okay that Emily had friends like this. That evening, though, I got a phone call from Maki's mother, who said, "Thank you so much for inviting Maki over. And she was so happy to have that delicious cake." When I ran across the other three mothers in the supermarket they also thanked me and told me how happy their girls had been to visit, so I rethought my first impression. Maybe these girls were better brought up than I'd imagined.

But truthfully you didn't enjoy yourselves, I know. The same was true for Akie.

Akie would always go with me wherever I invited her and did what she could to dress her best, but her shoes were still worn out. "Wouldn't you like to buy the boots I thought you should get?" I asked her, and she said, "They're wonderful, but kind of expensive. When I get paid for my part-time job, I'll buy some like them, ones I can afford." I hadn't known till then that she worked part-time at a restaurant.

"My parents back home are paying my tuition, which isn't cheap," she said, "so the least I can do is earn my own spending money."

I'd never once thought about tuition myself, and truthfully had no idea how much college cost. But my friends had always been that way. None of the girls I knew had part-time jobs. The only ones who did were poor girls we felt sorry for.

I felt sorry for Akie because she had to work. So I bought the boots for her. It wasn't her birthday or Christmas, but I felt that friends should simply want to make each other happy like that, regardless of whether it was for a special event. I attached a ribbon and a card that said *A sign of our friendship* and sent it to her apartment.

I couldn't wait to go to school. Would she have them on? I wondered. What outfit would she wear them with? And what would she say to me? But she wasn't wearing them. Maybe they hadn't arrived yet? I wondered. Or maybe she was saving them for a special occasion? As I was pondering this, she handed the boots back to me, still in the box. "I can't accept this kind of expensive shoes for no reason," she said. I couldn't believe it. I'd been positive she'd be overjoyed. "There's no need to hesitate," I told her, and she said she wasn't hesitating.

I gradually got more upset with her. "Why can't you understand my feelings?" I asked.

"It doesn't make sense for you to just refuse the boots," I told her. "I mean, I paid for meals for you, introduced you to my friends. If you're going to turn down the boots, then I want you to invite *me* out to eat, and introduce me to *your* friends. The food has to be something really good. And by friends, I mean boys. I introduced you to five boys, so you should do the same for me."

I wasn't really expecting she'd take me out to dinner or introduce me to some new boys. By insisting she do things I knew she couldn't, I was hoping to put her on the spot, hoping that would force her to back down and accept the gift.

But the next week she actually did invite me out to dinner. At a table in the back of an unappealing little *izakaya* restaurant, five boys were seated, waiting for me. And one of them was him.

He was a college student, two years older than Akie. He worked part-time in the kitchen at the same restaurant, and the other four boys were classmates of his in the education department.

"Akie told me she was having dinner with an amazing girl, so I hope you don't mind but I invited this lot over to join us."

He said this facetiously, but all of them struck me as earnest, formal types. The food was surprisingly good, and as we ate we began by asking each other where we were all from, those kinds of topics, but before thirty minutes were up I'd grown bored. I couldn't follow their conversation.

These education majors were pretty intense when it came to education in Japan. This was back in the days before anyone imagined the notion of "pressure-free" education. As they were talking they mentioned a friend who had failed the entrance exam, had a nervous breakdown, and almost tried to kill himself, and they discussed the need for a place where dropouts could get back on their feet.

Akie didn't venture an opinion but closely followed their conversation. The only one bored by it all was me. I mean, no one I knew ever had trouble with entrance exams or anything. They had a perfunctory test and interview before they entered elementary school, but after that it was smooth sailing through the system all the way into college, the so-called escalator system. None of my friends were especially remarkable students, but there weren't any dropouts, either.

The more heated the discussion got, the more it upset me. My boyfriends always talked about interesting topics so I wouldn't get bored, and I couldn't believe how inconsiderate these boys were. They said they were all from the countryside, and it made me wonder whether rural people were incapable of sophisticated conversation.

And as I sat there, bored, he was the one who spoke to me.

"All any of us know are rural public schools, but what kind of curriculum do they have at private girls' schools? Any unusual kinds of courses, or amusing teachers? Anything like that?"

Now, those were questions I could answer. I told him about a science teacher I had in middle school who was crazy about taking walks, who on sunny days liked to hold class outside. He taught us about the different plants and flowers in the four seasons, the names of various insects, why leaves turn red, when you could expect to see rainbows, how the walls of the school buildings seemed white but really weren't.... What surprised me was that it wasn't just this boy who'd asked me who listened intently to my story, but every one of his friends.

Kids from the countryside shouldn't find anything in nature so unusual, so what did they find so interesting? It was my turn to be surprised. As I expected, they all went on to reminisce about times back when they were children. All the things rural kids did—Kick the Can, Red Light Green Light, catching dragonflies and crayfish in rice fields, building secret forts in fields...

All kinds of games that I knew nothing about, though Emily played those games with the four of you.

I wanted to do the very best job I could of raising Emily. I felt it was my duty. So even before she could speak properly, I took her to supplementary after-school lessons and English conversation practice, plus piano and ballet. You might think I was some silly pushy parent, but Emily was very bright and sharp and learned everything quickly. She easily passed to get into a highly selective elementary school.

What would she become in the future? I wondered. I was sure Emily would be able to make anything come true—even things you could only dream about.

And then came the transfer to that rural town. My parents urged me to stay with Emily back in Tokyo. My husband wasn't opposed to the idea, but I decided we should go with him. This was a critical period in my husband's career—building this new factory meant a change in his position in the company—and I wanted to do what I could to support him. But even more important than that were Emily's feelings, since she said she wanted to go with her father. Emily really loved her papa.

My husband's assignment at the new factory was from three to five years, and I figured we could enjoy that time living in this country town with its pure air. So I didn't move there grudgingly, though things ended up as I wrote to you earlier.

After the move I regretted it every single day, but when I saw how Emily adapted I began to think that maybe it wasn't a bad decision.

My expectations of what I'd find in that town were way too optimistic. Even if there weren't any special or unusual programs for children, I was sure that at least there would be the same type of cram schools and other after-school programs that Emily had been attending in Tokyo. But all they had was a piano school. And the level of instruction there was so low—the teacher had graduated from some no-name music college and had no experience performing in competitions—I might as well have taught Emily piano myself. The local cram school allowed students starting in fifth and sixth grades and had classes in English and math, and was run by one teacher who, again, had only graduated from a second-rate school.

Any child raised in this kind of environment would have to be innately bright to be able to go on to a decent college. But more than that, I thought, it would take an inordinate amount of effort. It might lead to a nervous breakdown or, if one failed to get in, even to suicide. Some of the other mothers in our company housing early on sensed an impending crisis if they didn't take action and started taking their children to cram school in a larger city, a two-hour trip each way. They grumbled that the transportation expenses cost more than the tuition.

I felt as if I finally could understand what I'd heard over ten years before in that little *izakaya* about the pressures on children. So I decided not to push Emily too hard. We'd come out all this way to the country to live, so she should take advantage of it and do things she couldn't do back in the city. And Emily seemed to really enjoy life there.

She'd come home from school, drop off her backpack, then go right out to play until it got dark. After she came home, all she could talk about was the fun you'd all had together. How she'd seen some crayfish, played Kick the Can in the school grounds, and gone off into the hills, though what she did there was always *secret*.

She talked about all of you girls, too. Sae, she said, was quiet but reliable, Maki the hardest worker of all of you, Akiko was good at sports, and Yuka was skilled at handicrafts. Pretty amazing, isn't it, how closely Emily observed you all?

Quickly assimilating into life in the country, watching her new friends closely—she was the exact opposite of me. I'd always thought of her as my child alone, but now I began to see how his blood too ran through her.

The day after we went out to the *izakaya* Akie told me she would accept the boots.

"I'm sorry," she said, "I was just being stubborn. I'd like to wear these, if it's okay, as a sign of our friendship."

Ah, I thought, *so she really did want them after all*. Occasionally we went out together after that, but I no longer had the same desire to make her happy. And strangely enough, I no longer liked it when my boyfriends were nice to her. Akie was really popular among them, perhaps because she was the type of girl they'd never known before. One boy I was sure was head over heels just for me, it turned out, had asked Akie out behind my back.

But conversely, the boys Akie introduced me to started being very nice to me. At first it seemed they had me mistakenly pegged as an unapproachable rich girl. But once we'd started talking, they'd found me sociable and fun and said they'd like the same group to get together again. And we did, about once a week. One time we all went to one boy's hometown to swim at the seaside, and while we were there, too, they were very solicitous of me, making sure I wasn't bored or thirsty or anything.

Gradually I found it was more fun being with them than with my own boyfriends. It wasn't just because of how they treated me. It was more the vitality they had, how heatedly they debated education theory at every opportunity, that attracted me to them. And the one I was most attracted to was the boy who'd first spoken to me back at the *izakaya*.

At first he was the most considerate one toward me, but as all of them began to treat me kindly, he started to keep his distance. I realized that he was the one I most agreed with when they all debated, and that I was always watching him, and him alone. These education department students discussed education so intensely I was sure all of them wanted to become teachers, but he was the only one planning to. The others all wanted to become civil servants and change education policy that way. "But if you don't have experience in the classroom," he always countered, "how can you ever bring about a revolution in education?" The way he stood up to them made him even more manly and attractive in my eyes.

I liked him a lot but had no idea what to do about it. I was the type who always spoke my mind, but I'd never confessed my feelings for a man before. It had always been the man who told me his feelings, and up till then I'd never liked someone as much as I liked him.

If I had been certain he liked me, I might have been able to confess my feelings. But I wasn't sure if he did. So I enlisted Akie to help out. They worked at the same restaurant, so I asked her, when the two of them were alone, to sound him out about his feelings toward me.

To my great surprise, in a roundabout way she turned me down. "I'm just not sure about that—" she told me.

That upset me at first, but then I realized that if our positions were reversed and the answer came back negative, I would regret having accepted the request. If things were reversed... A thought struck me. First I'd get Akie and one of my boyfriends to fall for each other, then have her—as a way of thanking me—sound out the boy I was interested in about his feelings. I knew how conscientious she was and couldn't imagine her so absorbed in her own happiness that she'd turn me down if I asked for her help.

I asked one of the boys I knew to come see me, one I knew was interested in Akie. I didn't beat around the bush.

"You like Akie, right? No need to hesitate around me. Go for it. I'm sure Akie thinks you're nice. For one thing, you look like that singer she likes. The only reason she turned you down when you invited her out was because she's shy. She has a tendency to get more obstinate the happier she becomes. So just go for it. You know she can't hold her liquor. Tell her there's something about me that you want to talk with her about, and go out drinking, just the two of you. Once you get her drunk the rest should be easy."

My strategy paid off, and the man I had my eyes on and I became a couple. Or at least it seemed that way. It turned out I was the only one who was under that impression. It's always like that with me.

I was happy that you all became friends with Emily, and I was hoping that through you I would have a better relationship with all your mothers, and with others in town. But you never, ever accepted Emily.

And when she was murdered the reality of that became painfully clear.

The day we arrived in the town and I heard "Greensleeves" playing in the distance, I wondered what it was for. Was there some special event going on? The sad melody seemed to perfectly express how I was feeling. The woman from the factory office who was showing us around town explained that it was the time signal. At noon "Edelweiss," and at 6 p.m. "Greensleeves" played from the community center speakers. "When there are warnings issued," she went on, "or when there's some emergency, they'll broadcast the same way, so please listen to them carefully. Just that one little speaker is how they contact everyone in town." *That's how small the town is,* I thought, and felt miserable.

Still, the musical signal was convenient. I imagined that children, even if they had a watch on, might not look at it when they were having fun playing, but they'd hear the music. I used to tell Emily every time she went out to play, "When the music plays, come back home."

That day, too, as I was getting dinner ready I heard "Greensleeves." The factory was partly open, even during Obon, and my husband was at work, so I was alone at home. Just then the door intercom rang. *It must be Emily,* I thought, and opened the door, but there stood Akiko.

"Emily's dead!"

I thought it was some mean trick. From about two months before this, Emily had been occasionally asking me things like "What would you do if I died?" or "If something painful happens is it okay to die and then be reborn?" So my first thought was that she and her friends were trying to trick me, and that Emily was hiding behind the door waiting to see how I'd react. "Don't talk about dying, even as a joke," I'd told her several times. I was kind of upset.

But Emily wasn't hiding. *Was she in an accident?* I thought. *Where? At the school swimming pool? She knows how to swim, so how could that happen? Why Emily?*

My mind went blank. And right then what came to me was Akie's face.... I raced out of my house. *Don't take Emily away!*

When I got to the pool I heard a child crying or yelling, I wasn't sure which. It was Sae. She was crouched outside the changing rooms, head in her hands. "Where's Emily?" I asked, and she pointed behind her without looking up.

The changing room? Hadn't she fallen into the pool? I looked inside the dimly lit room and found Emily lying there, faceup on the drainboards, her head toward the door. She wasn't wet and didn't look hurt. Over her face was a handkerchief with a cute cat character on it. *Ah—so it is a trick, after all.* My legs felt about to give out.

Drained of the energy to get angry, I tugged off the handkerchief and found Emily's eyes open. "Just how long are you going to keep this up?" I asked, poking the tip of her nose. It felt cold. I held my palm out in front of her nose and mouth but felt no breath. I lifted her up and yelled her name again and again, in her ear but she didn't blink once. I shook her shoulders and screamed at her, but Emily never woke up.

I was in a state of disbelief. Even after the funeral I didn't want to accept that she was gone. This wasn't happening to us. I wished it were me who was dead.

A long time passed—I had no idea if it was day or night— and I asked my husband again and again, "Where is Emily?" I don't know how many times he answered in a quiet voice, "Emily is no longer with us." I'd never seen my husband cry before, but now when I saw the tears falling from his eyes it finally hit me that Emily was truly gone. "Why?" I repeated this question over and over. Why did Emily have to die? Why did she have to be strangled? Why did she have to be murdered? I wanted to hear this directly from the murderer himself. The murderer had to be caught and there wasn't a minute to spare.

I was sure they'd catch him soon. There were, after all, at least four eyewitnesses.

But all of you said the same thing: "We don't remember his face." I felt like slapping each one of you hard, one after the other. If you truly couldn't remember, there wasn't much we could do about it. But you didn't even seem to be trying hard to recall. And it wasn't just his face. You watched silently as Emily was led away by a strange man, then didn't go to check on her for over an hour. And not one of you seemed to regret that as you made your statements. Your friend died, yet not one of you cried.

Was it because you weren't sad?

As I looked at you I thought: *These girls realize something terrible's happened, but they don't feel sorry for Emily.* If it had been one of the other girls, not Emily, who'd been taken away they might not have let her go off by herself. Or else might have gotten worried and gone off earlier to check on her. You would have been sadder, would have done your utmost, for that girl's sake, to remember the murderer's face.

It wasn't just those girls, but their parents, too. My husband and I visited each family to ask them more about what had happened that day, but one of the parents, I can't recall which, muttered, "Who do you think you are, the police?" And one other parent yelled at us, "My child's been through enough already! Don't hurt her anymore." If we'd been a couple they knew from long ago and asked the same things, would they have reacted this way? I seriously doubt it.

Actually, everyone in town was the same. Onlookers from all over town gathered at the school that day, yet hardly any useful information came to light. Housewives I'd never seen before knew all about my asking for Camembert cheese at the supermarket, so how could there be not a speck of information, or any leads, about the murderer? If it had been a local girl who'd been killed, there would have been a flood of leads about various unsavory types.

On top of that were the public-address announcements blaring over the loudspeaker. For a while after the murder, at times when children were going to and from school they'd have announcements like: "Good children never do things alone, but always do things with someone from their family or a friend." "If a stranger talks to you do not go with him." But why didn't they also announce something like "If anyone has any information that could help in the crime that took place recently, no matter how small, please contact the police"?

No one—*no one*—mourns Emily's death. No one understands the pain I felt at having my child killed.

There were so few leads about the man who murdered her that for a time I even suspected that the four of you had killed her. You all killed her and all agreed on a story you made up about a criminal who didn't exist. You didn't want to be caught up in a lie so you said you couldn't remember what he looked like. And everyone in town knew this and was protecting you.

I was the only one who didn't know what was going on. Me, the one left all alone.

You appeared to me in my dreams, as every night a different one of you strangled Emily. Murdered her while you let out a hideous laugh. And turning your malicious face to me, you said, over and over in chorus, *I don't remember his face.*

Before I realized what I was doing, I had run out of the house, barefoot, clutching a knife.

My husband chased after me. "What do you think you're doing?" he asked, and I said, "I'm getting revenge for Emily." "But they haven't found the murderer yet," he said. "Those children—*they're* the ones who killed her!" I screamed back. "It can't be them. I mean, look…," my husband countered but faltered, not wanting to say aloud that Emily had been sexually assaulted.

I didn't care. It was them—*those girls* who did it!

I screamed and screamed…but don't remember anything after that. I might have fainted, might have been held down by other residents of the company apartment, might have been given a sedative. It's all a blur.

Afterward I couldn't get by without sedatives, and my husband said it would be best if I went back to my parents' place and rested for a time. But I refused. If we hadn't come to this town, Emily wouldn't have been killed. It was this town that had killed her. I loathed the town but didn't leave it because if I did everyone would forget all about the murder. And the murderer would never be caught.

And I hadn't lost all hope in you girls. As I gradually recovered I remembered you were just ten-year-old girls after

all. Pushing children that young—driving them to *remember!*
remember!—wouldn't help. Those girls themselves, I thought,
had not fully recovered. Once they were back to normal they
might remember something. And might finally mourn Emily.
Maybe one of them would even show up for a memorial service
for her, to light incense and pray.

Still, three years passed and you all just kept repeating the
same thing. I was sure now that you four had killed her. That's
why I said what I did.

"I will never forgive you, unless you find the murderer before the statute of limitations is up. If you can't do that, then
atone for what you've done, in a way I'll accept. If you don't
do either one, I'm telling you here and now—I *will* have revenge on each and every one of you."

Maybe I'm the worst adult imaginable for saying something
like this to young girls, girls barely in junior high. But unless I
said something shocking like that, I thought, you would forget
all about Emily. And you four were the only eyewitnesses.

And I was sure that even though I'd said that to you, the day
after I left town you'd forget all about the murder.

That's why—though I haven't forgotten Emily for a
second—I decided to wipe that town totally out of my mind.

In Tokyo I had family and friends who consoled me. And
there were lots of places I could go to take my mind off my sorrow. But the one who comforted me the most might have been
Takahiro. Other than Sae, you probably don't know who I'm
talking about.

When he lived in that town, he was the only child who was
concerned about me.

My husband's cousin and his wife came to town at the same time we did to work at the Adachi Manufacturing plant. They might be relatives, but the wife also worked, and the couple didn't seem to get along well, so we didn't see them much. As for Takahiro, I heard he was a bright little boy, but there was a cold look in his eyes and he was the kind of child who, even if you happened to run across him in the hallway of the apartment building, wouldn't say hello.

Yet after the incident he came by himself to my place.

"I am truly sorry that I couldn't do anything to help after that awful thing happened. I was back in Tokyo when it all took place," he said. "I'm thinking I'll ask the kids at school to see if they know anything that might be a lead, so I was wondering if you could tell me about the day it happened. Just what you feel comfortable talking about."

Before this, though, he went over to the tablet set up to memorialize Emily, lit a stick of incense, and said a silent prayer for her. He was the only one ever to do that, and it made me very happy. He asked about the connection with the French Doll Robbery incident, but we had nothing to do with French dolls—the townspeople had seemed to have jumped the gun in linking the crimes, but no evidence had surfaced proving they were committed by the same person. That's what I told him.

After this he stopped by our house occasionally. He never had any important information to share, but I was happy that he showed concern about the murder, and about how I was doing.

Both our families returned to Tokyo at the same time, and back home he continued to stop by every once in a while.

"Your house is on the way back from school and I just thought I'd drop by. I know you'll always treat me to something good to eat. I'm sorry."

He sounded quite apologetic, but I enjoyed having Takahiro over. All he did was tell me about things happening at his school, but somehow it cheered me up.

Before Emily had even entered elementary school I had a discussion once with one of the other mothers I had gotten to know at the private cram school Emily attended. We were talking about which we found more adorable—boys or girls. Naturally I said girls. "You can dress them up in cute clothes, talk with them like your friends, go out shopping together." The other mother said, "I used to think so too. But now I'm not so sure."

She had two children, an older girl and a boy Emily's age. This is what she told me:

"Before I had children I thought I wanted a girl. I figured even after she grew up, we could be friends. So when I had a girl I was overjoyed. But it was after I had a boy that I understood. A girl is, after all, a friend. That's fun, but girls compete with each other. When I see her whispering some secret to my husband, it upsets me. A boy, though, is more like a lover than a friend. Even though it's your own child, it's still the opposite sex. So you don't compete with each other. You want to do whatever you can for him, unconditionally. And all it takes to cheer you up is having him say a few kind words to you. I'm looking forward to hearing from my daughter about boyfriends someday, but I imagine I'll have mixed feelings when my son grows up and tells me about his girlfriend."

Hearing this, I imagined if Emily had been a boy. When she was born I thought she looked just like me, but as she grew older I was startled sometimes at how much she resembled her father. If she'd been a boy I probably would have given her a hug because of that. And I might have felt even more strongly that I had to take very, very good care of her.

But none of that matters now. Boy or girl, as long as they lived that would be enough for me.

I've gotten off topic, but I started to feel as if Takahiro were my own son. I asked him if he had a girlfriend, and he laughed and said a couple, but nothing serious, deflecting the question. But it was enough to give me mixed feelings.

Sometimes he visited friends in that town, and through that caught an occasional kernel of news about you four. You were all living ordinary lives, he said, nothing special to report. *Just as I suspected*, I thought at first, and this made me angry. But gradually I came to accept that this was okay.

The one I should be angry at is the murderer. Those girls have their own lives to live.

If Emily had been in your situation I'm sure I would have told her to forget all about the murder. How many years did it take for me to finally arrive at this realization? I wonder. I truly came to believe it was good that you could live normal lives again.

Takahiro stopped going back to that town and I heard no more news about you and stopped thinking about you. *That's how you forget about things*, I thought.

It was the beginning of spring this year when Takahiro came to our home and said there was a girl he wanted to seriously go out with, and asked us to act as go-betweens and set up the *omiai* meeting with her. It made me a little sad to think of him getting married, but I was overjoyed that he would ask me and my husband to take on such an important task. My husband liked Takahiro, and when he heard that the girl worked in a company that was a client of his company, he eagerly accepted, saying he would get in touch with her superiors in her workplace.

But when I heard the girl's name I was shocked. *One of those four girls?* I couldn't believe my ears.

At first Takahiro apologized for it and explained that when he visited the town he started to get interested in Sae, that at the end of the year he'd happened to see her again in Tokyo with her work colleagues and felt as if it was fate that he ran into her again. Before he left he apologized again. "I'm very sorry if I've stirred up painful memories for you, Auntie, and for Uncle," he said.

Painful? I didn't feel that way. *So Takahiro is that age now, is he,* I thought, and was surprised to think that the girls the same age as Emily were now old enough to get married. I couldn't believe that that much time had passed.

If only Emily had lived…She's the one I should have brought together with the person she loved. I should have protected her until that day.

"There's no need to apologize," I told Takahiro. "When you love a person you don't need someone else's permission to be with them."

The two of them had their *omiai,* began seeing each other regularly, and then decided to marry. Since the girl was one of you four, I was half resigned to not being invited to the wedding, but my husband and I were the first ones Takahiro invited. "Sae really hopes you'll attend," he told me.

Sae had grown so pretty it was hard to believe she was once a child from that rustic little town. Dressed in a white wedding gown, surrounded by friends from work wishing her well, she had a radiant smile.

But the instant she saw me, her smile vanished and she looked at me fearfully. A natural response, I guess, when suddenly confronted on the happiest day of your life with someone who reminds you of a past tragedy.

"Forget about what happened," I told her, "and be happy."

"Thank you," she said, tears running down her cheeks. I felt a weight lifted off my shoulders too. Though I couldn't say this to all of you—these words I should have said a long time ago—I was so glad I was able to say it to her then.

And yet, Sae went on to murder Takahiro.

A terrible series of crimes had begun.

When my husband first told me about the murder, I knew there had to be some mistake. Less than a month after being so happy at her wedding ceremony, the bride—Sae—killed Takahiro? Wasn't it an accident? A burglar broke in, perhaps, and Takahiro was killed trying to protect Sae? And she said, "I'm the one who killed him"?

It happened in a far-off country so I wasn't able to see Takahiro's body, just to hear, indirectly, that Sae had confessed to the police to murdering her husband. I couldn't accept that he was dead.

Takahiro, who was like a son to me...Takahiro, the only one who ever consoled me after Emily was murdered...

If I could have seen the body with my own eyes, I might have been able to truly despise Sae for snatching away my beloved son. But before that could happen, I received a letter.

As I read the long letter I realized I'd been wrong all this time. I couldn't believe that Emily's murder would weigh so heavily on her. For a while afterward she couldn't help but feel fear, compounded by the fact that the murderer was still on the loose. But normally as time passed you should be able to forget that. Yet Sae couldn't, and the murder held her prisoner to a fear so great it affected her health. I'm sure she felt a gaze on her at times.

It was hard to believe that Takahiro had gone to that town in order to keep watch over Sae. And that he was the one who stole the French dolls. I didn't want to believe it, yet I don't think Sae was lying in her letter. Still, I don't want you to label Takahiro as a pervert so quickly. I understand his feelings very well.

Like me, he was very lonely in that town. You have to realize that, because of problems in his family, he no longer knew how to form relationships with people, and that would include the children in town. So he fell in love with dolls and had his eye constantly on a girl who resembled them. Don't condemn him for this. No matter the motivation for wanting her to be his, I know he wanted to treasure Sae for the rest of his life.

And Sae, too, tried to understand and accept the way he was. Which is why she decided it was all right for her body to become fully a woman's. But at that very moment a tragedy occurred.

Was it all my fault?

Sae took the words I told you all that day as a firm *promise*. That's why she couldn't forget the murder, why her mind and body both were held in thrall to it. And as she tried to forget the promise and everything that went with it, suddenly there I was, at her wedding, the happiest day of her life, to remind her of it all over again.

I told her to forget the murder, but for her that may have been, conversely, the trigger that made her realize that the murder was fading from her memory.

Am I to blame for Takahiro's death? Was I the one who bound her to Emily's death?

That's what I wanted to know. No, that's not it, really. What I wanted was for her to *deny* it. To tell me "No, it's not because of you." That's what I wanted to hear. If the other three girls had moved on from the murder and were living normal lives now, I could put Sae down as a special case, the one exception.

Apart from this, I felt I had to tell all of you, since I suspected, at least from what she said in the letter, that you didn't know how Sae felt after the murder. So I made copies of her letter without her permission and sent them to you. Was that wrong? I don't know. But I thought that you three—of all people—you who had all been part of the same murder, would forgive me.

No, it's that I simply couldn't bear the guilt alone for what happened to her. That's the real reason I sent you all the letter

I received from Sae. Why not append a message from me, too? It's because I had no idea what to say.

The three of you are all okay, I assume? I couldn't write something like that.

Don't do anything stupid. Even less could I have written something like that.

But I should have. Because I didn't write anything and just forwarded the letter without comment, Maki, too, was driven into a corner. By me.

I first heard about the incident with Maki on the TV news. I couldn't imagine that she had been part of it. I mean, it took place in a far-off seaside town, and even though it involved, shockingly, a man breaking into an elementary school, only one child was hurt badly so it wasn't covered all that extensively. But the fact that it took place at an elementary school swimming pool spurred me on to learn more.

It might not have been big news on TV, but it was all over the Internet and weekly news magazines. One teacher stood up to the intruder while the second ran away, and the former was a female teacher while the latter was an athletic male teacher. Perfect fodder for a splashy story for the Internet to play up.

Both teachers' real names and photos were made public. When I saw that one of them was Maki I was shocked. But it also made me happy.

Ah, I thought, *so she's living an ordinary life*—in fact had worked hard to carve out her own life. Becoming a teacher and protecting young children was not something she could have done if she were still seized with fear over the murder. I concluded that Sae was indeed the exception, a basically weak-willed person, and that it wasn't all my fault.

But that feeling of relief was short-lived. As I searched for more news on the incident one day, I ran across a weird item.

Maki was a murderer, it said.

On the TV news it said that the intruder died because he stabbed his own leg and fell into the pool, but in this Internet report it said that when the intruder tried to climb out of the pool Maki kicked him repeatedly and thus killed him.

I know you can't believe everything you read online, but I couldn't totally ignore it, and I decided to phone Maki's elementary school. They must have had plenty of prank calls, for the first thing they did was ask my name and affiliation, which threw me a little. But I was determined to learn the facts, so I went ahead and gave them my name, and since I had no title I gave my husband's company and position and said I was the mother of one of Maki's friends. They told me Maki was on campus and they'd pass along my message.

I was the one who had called, yet the whole thing had me flustered for a moment. There was so much I wanted to ask, but where to start?

As I was pondering this, Maki came on the line.

"We're holding an unscheduled PTA meeting the day after tomorrow," she said. "I have something I'd like you to hear, so I hope you'll attend."

She hung up right after this, but I was relieved to hear how calm she sounded. A person who'd kicked an intruder to death wouldn't be that calm, and the fact that she'd answered the phone meant she hadn't been arrested. Those online reports must be nonsense, I decided.

I took the Shinkansen train all the way to her town to attend because I wanted to ask her about Sae. I knew Maki was going through a lot, but I felt that someone like her, who'd lived a decent, upright life, would listen.

But what Maki said at the meeting threw me even deeper into a pit of shame and guilt.

I was startled from the very beginning. She said that right after the murder she remembered the murderer's face. *If that's true, why didn't you ever say anything? You'd gone home before any of the other children, but none of the adults would have blamed you for that. Instead, I wish you had told what the murderer looked like. If you had, I'm sure I would never have been able to thank you enough. And I might not have subjected you, or the other girls as well, to those words I said, three years after Emily was killed....*

But as I listened to Maki now, I couldn't blame her. I knew that she, too, was held captive by Emily's murder, and by my words, in a way that went beyond fear.

If I hadn't said what I did, and hadn't forwarded Sae's letter, Maki would still have protected her children. But she might not have delivered the final blow to finish off the intruder.

As I sat there in the last row in the gym, I was stricken by the series of crimes that had occurred, and I wanted to dash out of there. But I couldn't even stand up. For I had just heard an unbelievable name.

As Maki kicked the intruder, she remembered a person resembling the murderer from fifteen years ago. I found it incredible that his name would come up. And, she added, somewhat ambiguously, there's someone who resembles him even more.

I think this is what she wanted to say:

"The murderer looked a lot like Emily."

I can only hope this was some misunderstanding on her part.

Maybe when she kicked that intruder, she remembered Emily's face, and that gave her the illusion that she remembered the murderer's.

And then the face of a famous man who resembled Emily came to her. That makes sense. She might have forced herself to have that impression.

But there was something I had to do before thinking about the murderer.

I had to put a stop to this series of crimes.

I decided to summarize what Maki had said at the meeting, and this time add my own message to it. That same night all of what Maki had said was on the website of a sleazy weekly magazine. My name was given as Ms. A, the *mystery adviser,* as they put it.

I had an acquaintance delete that, but before that I made two copies of the article and put them in envelopes.

I've forgiven all of you.

That's the message I appended to it. So don't do anything dreadful. Killing a different man in place of the murderer is *not* a form of penance. I could only hope that the rest of the girls would hear my prayer.

And yet next Akiko killed someone. And that, too, was in

the same town, and almost unimaginably, the victim was her own brother....

This wasn't the time to write letters anymore.

I set off for that town.

Akiko killed her brother in order to protect a little girl.

What I should apologize to Akiko for is not those words I told her three years after Emily's murder, but what happened immediately afterward. The instant I heard that Emily had been killed, I may well have shoved Akiko aside. Everything went blank before me at that moment and I honestly can't recall. But I want you to know this: I didn't push Akiko down because I hated her. And of course I never thought Akiko deserved to be treated that way.

But it was me, I think, who drove her to do what she did.

She never read either of the two letters. She thought the letters were reminders of the promise she'd made. Maybe that's why her little niece and Emily overlapped in her mind.

Then what should I have done?

Fortunately, when I got in touch with Yuka's family from the hospital where Akiko was hospitalized, I learned that Yuka's apartment was only three stops away by train, so I decided to go see her directly. Yuka's mother hadn't heard my voice in over ten years and at first didn't realize it was me, but once I told her my name she seemed to make the connection.

"I understand exactly how much you want them to arrest the murderer before the statute of limitations runs out," Yuka's mother said. "But Yuka is going to have a baby very soon. It's a critical time for her. I'd prefer that you leave her alone." She was pretty upset.

With what happened with Sae, and Maki and Akiko both wary of men ever since the murder, it really surprised me to hear that Yuka was pregnant.

Then Yuka's okay, I decided. I knew very well how women got stronger when they got pregnant. If you have another life growing inside you, you can put up with painful things that, on your own, you couldn't. The child inside your womb is more important than yourself, and as long as that maternal instinct arose I was sure she wouldn't be taking any rash actions.

Still, I couldn't just go back to Tokyo.

I had a photograph I had to have her look at. "It's just one photo I'd like her to take a look at," I told Yuka's mother, and somehow persuaded her to give me the address of Yuka's apartment and her cell phone number.

I'd brought the photo with me. I was hoping that Maki was mistaken, but the name she gave was a name connected with something I deeply regretted in my past, and I just had to know.

Naturally, I planned to show it to Akiko, too. There was a possibility that though she said she didn't remember the man's face, in fact she did. But she told me that not only didn't she remember his face, she couldn't recall any other details about him. So showing the photo to her would be pointless, which actually made me feel a little relieved. Even so, she mentioned the same name.

She said that on the day of the murder her cousin and his girlfriend, who were visiting town, saw a man who resembled him at the station. The cousin said the man was his girlfriend's teacher back in elementary school.

I was afraid to be alone. The reason I went to see Yuka wasn't so she would tell me he wasn't the murderer, but more to have someone hear about the sin I had committed in my own past. But it wasn't the time or place, and I didn't talk about it.

That's why I'm writing about it here.

After I started going out with him, Akie and I grew apart. Not that we quarreled or didn't get along anymore, but as seniors we were in different seminars and I didn't go to school as often as before.

He was in his second year of teaching at an elementary school and I started spending all my time at his place, as if I were his wife. While he was at work I did the cleaning and prepared meals, totally absorbed in the kind of housework I'd never done before. I mentioned wanting to get married and living together.

"After you graduate I'd like to formally go to visit your family," he said, and I was overjoyed. His words alone should have been enough for me, but I was impatient and said I couldn't rely on a verbal promise alone. So he used his meager bonus from work to buy me a ring. An engagement ring with my birthstone, a ruby. I couldn't have been happier, and while he was out I'd try the ring on over and over, then take it off and polish it.

And then one day my hand slipped and the ring fell beneath the desk. And that's when I spotted a notebook I'd never seen before protruding from a drawer. It had been pushed to the very back and stuck out all the more. A secret notebook, it looked like.

Maybe it's just some study notes, I thought, and I pulled it out and opened it. Because I wanted to know everything about him. But I soon regretted opening it. The notebook was his diary. If it had been an ordinary diary I would have enjoyed going ahead and reading it, feeling a twinge of guilt perhaps. If he'd written about me, that would have made me happy to read it.

But the diary was full of his longing for another woman, someone he couldn't let go of.

Is the promise we made then not forever?

Why did your feelings change so suddenly? Why didn't you say anything?

I know you betrayed me, but I can't help thinking of you every single night.

I knew right away this *you* he wrote about wasn't me. Because I was there, with him every day. The dates in the diary overlapped with when he started seeing me, and I felt horribly betrayed. I left his apartment, went back home, and shut myself away in my room. I really did start to feel sick and took to my bed.

I had no appetite and felt feverish, as if I were on a rolling boat and seasick. I'd never imagined that finding out he loved someone other than me would cause this much hurt. *Am I this weak a woman?* I wondered. I'd run out after reading halfway, but maybe I should have read the diary to the very end. Then at least I might discover the name of this other woman. Find out who she is, and if I felt she was no match for me, it would be okay, wouldn't it, since he'd promised to marry me?

Maybe Akie knows who it is. I can ask her if, back when they worked together at the restaurant, there was any other woman who came to see him.

I phoned her right away. Quite a while before, she'd told me that things hadn't worked out with one of the boyfriends I'd arranged for her to date, so I figured she'd understand how I feel and kindly hear me out.

Akie was at home in the apartment she lived in alone. I'd visited her only once and remembered it as a dim, spare, lonely little place. She said she was writing up her résumé so she could find a job after school.

"Asako, you're not going to go out for job interviews? Oh, right—you don't need to. You can use your family's connections to get in wherever you want. I envy you. So, why are you calling?"

I hadn't heard my friend's voice in some time, but it sounded cold, as if she was trying to reject me. Her search for a job probably wasn't going well, and she was on edge, but still it angered me that she would use this tone with me when I was feeling so down. That's why I went ahead and said what I did.

"You're right. I mean, I'm going to get married to him. After I graduate we're going to officially announce it to my parents, and he gave me an engagement ring, too. I told him not to go to the trouble since it's so expensive, but he insisted I accept it. I haven't told this to anyone else yet, but I think I'm pregnant. So we might not wait until I graduate to get married.

I'm so happy, Akie, and it's all because of you, since you're the one who introduced us."

I'm not sure myself why I said I was pregnant then, just because I'd been feeling a little under the weather. I might have been trying to reassure myself. Akie remained silent. So I went ahead and babbled on and on about the things I did to take care of him, movies we'd seen together recently, and so on. And finally Akie spoke up.

"If it's okay, why don't you come over right now? I want to hear it all from you directly, not over the phone. And you can show me your engagement ring, too. It must be gorgeous."

I looked at the clock and saw it was after nine. Going out this late was a bother, but all this talking about my love had perked me up and I thought it was worth going there, if only to show off my ring. "After I get ready I'll be right over," I told her, and hung up.

It was only about thirty minutes to her apartment by taxi, but with the weekend and the crowded roads it took nearly an hour to get there. I knocked at the door of her place but there was no answer. Thinking maybe she hadn't heard, I tried the doorknob, and the door wasn't locked so I went in. Beyond the tiny entrance there was just one six-mat room and I saw her immediately.

She was collapsed on the bed, which was covered in blood. She'd cut her wrists. It didn't occur to me to call an ambulance. I was terrified and instead used her phone to call him.

"Come over right now," I said. He said he'd gone out drinking with a colleague and was exhausted. Could we make it tomorrow?

"You need to come right this minute. Come to Akie's apartment. She—she killed herself."

He hung up almost before I'd gotten the words out. *He's coming,* I thought vacantly as I sat beside Akie. That's when I noticed an unopened letter on top of her desk.

Addressed to me, maybe? I mean, Akie was the one who'd asked me over. I opened it to find a single sheet of stationery.

Hiroaki, I love you forever.

What is *this? Akie loved* him? *Could he have also loved her? Did Akie kill herself to spite me?* But had she really planned to die? If I hadn't been caught in a traffic jam and gotten here earlier, maybe she would have failed in her attempt.... *What should I do? He'll be here soon....*

I stuck the letter in my bag and ran out of the apartment. A resident of another unit was just coming home and I had them call an ambulance, but Akie was beyond saving. And he never came.

Maybe unable to find a taxi, maybe wanting to get over to Akie's as fast as he could, he had borrowed a car from a colleague in the same apartment building and driven toward Akie's place. But on the way he got in an accident.

It was a minor accident, a fender bender, and though no one was hurt he'd been drinking beforehand. And naïve me had no idea of the consequences.

If a teacher was arrested for DUI he would be dismissed in disgrace from his position and lose his job.

All that had suddenly befallen us frightened me, and I ran away from him.

As I walked to Yuka's apartment he was all I thought about. Did he kill Emily? But *why*, ten years later, and in that town? I had kept Akie's letter all those years. People around her at the time were sure that Akie had done it because she'd been turned down for all the companies she applied for. Employment neurosis, they called it. Don't misunderstand me. She was an earnest, outstanding young woman. If she were alive today I'm sure she'd be hired by a large corporation and become a top career woman. But back then, society didn't accept women like her. Someone like her from the back of nowhere, with no connections, wouldn't be able to even get a job doing clerical work, let alone with any prospects of promotion. They would have tossed her résumé in the reject file with barely a glance, before she even took the written exam or had an interview.

But truly she was more intelligent than any woman I've ever known. It was no wonder he fell in love with her. One of them should have told me about it. If they had, I wouldn't have done anything to stop them. I had no interest in any man who was in love with some other woman.

Somehow he must have found out what I'd done. Tearing them apart, driving the woman he loved to suicide, then running away. *Now that I think of it, isn't there a town near here with the same name as the one Akie said she came from?...*

As these thoughts were vacantly whirling around in my head, I walked from the station and arrived at Yuka's apartment. With that fixed stare of hers behind her glasses, maybe she did remember what the murderer looked like. I was picturing showing her, at this late date, a photo of him, and her saying "No, I don't think it's him," and was about to start up the stairs when I heard a man and a woman arguing. *What awful timing I have,* I thought, and hid in the shadows of the bushes and saw them appear on the stairs above me.

It was Yuka and a man. And Yuka looked about to be knocked over.

I quickly pulled out my cell phone and punched in Yuka's number, which I had in my contacts list. The theme song for a detective drama I was familiar with rang out and the man fell down the stairs. It was dark so I couldn't really see how he happened to fall. When I saw how calm she was when she called for the ambulance, I decided not to show myself. If she had fallen apart and collapsed in tears, I probably would have come out to her right away. But I couldn't bring myself to when she was that calm.

After she climbed aboard the ambulance, I hailed a taxi.

After I had been in the taxi a while and had calmed down, this thought hit me: *The last girl has finally done it.* If only I hadn't hidden, hadn't called her on the phone but had confronted her and told her "Stop it!" I felt regret, but I knew all too well that remorse after the fact was pointless.

Maybe I had gradually resigned myself to my fate. Or perhaps I had a premonition sprouting inside me that the series of tragedies that had taken place would, in the end, come my way.

That was probably why I could listen so calmly to the end of Yuka's story.

I had had no idea about Emily playing in that abandoned cottage. Though I do remember the ring going missing.

I couldn't bring myself to throw away the ring he gave me, or Akie's suicide note. I'd carefully placed it in a box and put it in the back of the closet, but when I was putting things away after we moved, Emily happened to see that box and opened it up. "That's so pretty," she said, eyes narrowed as she opened the ring case. "Why is this in here?" she asked, to which I immediately answered, "Because this is going to be yours, Emily."

"Then let me have it now," Emily said. "Someday," I said, "when the time comes." And I didn't give it to her. She pouted a bit, though she seemed to like the notion of a secret promise. She always liked those kinds of things.

Someday. When the time comes. When the time came that I had to tell her who her real father was.

After I ran away from him I started going out with my old friends. That felt like where I really belonged. I didn't have the strength to mourn a girl who had killed herself while simultaneously propping up a man who'd lost his job. There was no way I could share a miserable life with him. And the person my friends introduced me to then became my present husband.

His grandfather was the founder of Adachi Manufacturing and he'd joined the company himself five years before. I thought his eyes were cold and that he was a little scary, and when I asked him, "Are there any other girls you like?" he said, "If there were I wouldn't be here." "Then I'll be happy to go out with you," I said, bowing. He laughed, cheerfully. "Same here," he said, holding out his hand. We shook hands on it, and that's when we started dating.

I think it was on our third date when we were out on a drive. I suddenly felt sick, asked him to pull over, and got out. I felt dizzy and collapsed on the spot. When I woke up I was in a room in the nearest private hospital, and he was seated beside me. I quickly tried to sit up but he told me to lie down and rest.

"It's not good for the baby you're carrying," he said.

I felt about to collapse again. A boyfriend I had never slept with was announcing I was pregnant. *It's all over with us*, I figured. *This is my punishment for having run away.* God wasn't going to forgive me for forgetting everything and trying to be the only one who ended up happy. I was more concerned at this point about my life from then on than with my relationship with Adachi. What would my parents say when they found out? And other people I knew? I knew I couldn't make it on my own.

Assuming that my relationship with Adachi was over, I told him all about the baby's father. Without touching on Akie.

When I'd finished, Adachi said something that bowled me over.

"Let's get married," he said. "I'd like you to have the child as mine."

He didn't say this out of love for me. He wasn't able to have children himself, probably because of a bout of mumps when he was in college. He hadn't been tested at a hospital, he said, so it wasn't totally certain that was the cause. But it was certain his sperm count was zero. He'd used his own company's test kit, so there was no mistake.

He was ambitious. He was a grandson of the founder, but he was the son of the founder's second son, and the older brother's son would be the one set to inherit the company. But he was more able, he felt, than that other son—his cousin—and he swore to himself that he would someday become the company president. But one day, half jokingly, he tested himself and found out he was sterile. Would people allow a person who couldn't have any descendants to be the heir? Ever since then, he seemed to have given up on the idea of heading the company. Even after his friends introduced me to him, he said he didn't intend to marry me.

And then he heard from the doctor that I was pregnant.

We made a deal. He'd provide a stable life for me, and I'd help him win the trust of those around him.

He quickly registered me in his family register as his wife. When the baby was born, presumably early but still at normal weight for full term, we told people we'd slept together from the start. And we named the baby girl Emily. My husband's grandfather, the founder of the company, named her. Apparently it was the name of a girl he fell in love with when he was studying abroad.

But I always felt that Emily was mine alone.

Not to imply that we weren't loved. Adachi took good care of me and loved Emily like his own daughter.

I had no inkling that day was coming. So that ring should still have been in the box with Akie's note in the back of the closet in our company housing apartment where I'd put it.

One day there was a company party, and I thought I'd wear a string of pearls and took my jewelry box from the back of the closet. And I noticed that the lid of the other box was askew.

I took it out and found the ring, along with the case, gone. As well as the note from Akie. The next day the ring was back, but the note wasn't.

"If Daddy found out you loved another man he'd be sad," Emily said, "so I thought I'd better hide it somewhere outside the house. I could get back the ring, but the note got thrown away. I'm so sorry. I'm so sorry."

As she stood there, crying and telling me this, I felt a wave of love for her. She'd mistakenly thought I'd written that note, though my handwriting was never as beautiful as that.

Emily had hidden the ring and note in the abandoned cottage. And as he was searching for a suitable building to use for his free school, he discovered it there. Maybe he was searching for a place there, thinking that, as he rebuilt his life, he'd do it in a place that had some connection with Akie. I'm sure he was shocked at what he found. He just opened a cookie tin he happened to run across, only to find a ring he remembered all too well. And a suicide note addressed to him.

I think he realized right away that Akie had written it.

After this he probably started investigating things. He'd lost the woman he loved, and the job he'd poured all his passion into—should I be blamed for that, too? Where was the woman who'd stolen away everything precious to him and run away, and what was she doing now? And what was precious to her?

Emily was murdered all because of me.

The four of you just happened to get involved. And what I

said to you was unforgivable. You took it to heart and led me to the murderer.

It's my turn now to do penance for you.

After I left Yuka I went to see him.

Until I arrived at the free school, which had been widely reported about in weekly magazines, my thoughts were about *penance*. About what I should do for the sake of you four.

Should I hire a top lawyer and have all four of you declared innocent? Should I help pay for your living expenses? Or pay you compensation money?

But doing any of that, I thought, would only earn your contempt.

What I had to do was none of those things, but rather to confess my sins, and tell the murderer, Hiroaki Nanjo, the truth.

You are Emily's father.

And I did. I told him that clearly.

I think you all know, through TV and the newspapers, what happened to him afterward. And I think you can understand how I feel about that, even if I don't write about it here.

I wonder if you have it in your hearts to forgive me.

And whether you are freed now from the curse that's held you in its spell for so many years.

Asako Adachi

The Final Chapter

A summer sky as twilight approaches.

They pass the locked back gate and clamber over the chain-link fence. Two people.

One of them carries an old, well-used volleyball, the other a small bouquet of flowers.

They head to the school playground.

"They talk about beefing up anticrime measures, but it's still easy to get in.... Speaking of which, is it hard for you to be here? You don't feel traumatized or anything?"

"I'm okay. What about you? Can you see things all right today?"

"No problem. But I'm not confident we can do a hundred times in a row the very first time."

"We'll try as long as we need to. Like on that day..."

The two of them lay their bags down at their feet and face each other.

A white ball goes back and forth between them.

One, two, three...fifty-one, fifty-two, fifty-three...ninety-one, ninety-two...

"Ninety-three...Ah! Sorry!"

The mis-hit ball rolls away.

A ball rolling away. Five children chasing it.

A man in work clothes, Hiroaki Nanjo, picks up the ball.

"I'm here to check the ventilation fan for the changing rooms in the pool, but totally forgot to bring a ladder. We just need to tighten a few screws, so could one of you ride piggyback on my shoulders and help out?"

The shortest girl takes the ball from him.

"To ride piggyback I should do it since I'm the smallest."

The tallest girl steps forward.

"It'd be a problem if you can't reach the fan, so should I go since I'm the tallest?"

A girl wearing glasses in the back interrupts.

"But can either of you twist a screw? I'm really good at it."

"But what'll you do if the screw is too tight? I'm strong so I think I could handle it." The biggest girl says this proudly.

Nanjo looks at the five children one by one.

"Can't be someone either too small or too big.... I wouldn't want your glasses to fall off, and you look a little heavy, maybe...."

He walks over to the most intelligent-looking child, Emily.

"You're just right."

Emily looks back anxiously at the other four.

The tallest girl claps her hands and speaks loudly.

"Then let's all help!"

The other three children agree.

Nanjo is nonplussed. But still he smiles.

"Thank you, but the changing room is cramped and if too many go it'll be hard to work. I wouldn't want anyone to get hurt. So why don't you stay here. We'll be done real soon. And afterward I'll buy you all ice cream."

The four children are delighted.

Nanjo takes Emily by the hand and leaves.

Not knowing they are related, father and child—

The two of them pick up the ball and start passing it back and forth again.

"...One hundred!"

They take deep breaths.

They pick up their bags, head for the gym, and sit down side by side on the steps to the entrance.

"So what did that murder mean for us, anyway?"

"And the fifteen years after..."

"When I was reading that long letter from her—more of a memoir, really, since it was so long—it made me wonder what the point of my life has been."

"Maybe I was a victim. And because I felt that way, that's why her words weighed so heavily on me. Even so, we were just caught up in it all."

"Normally if you'd done such awful things in your past,

wouldn't you ask yourself, right after the murder, whether it was *your* fault?"

"Yeah, but not thinking that was her way of dealing with life. If someone did ask themselves that, maybe it would mean they really didn't have anything like that in their past?"

"I suppose.... But I can't really blame her. She's the one who suffered the most. And it's also thanks to her that I can live an ordinary life now."

"They charged you with inflicting bodily injury, but you got probation, right?"

"Right. The cause of death was loss of blood, and he'd stabbed himself. I never touched the knife, and kicking him in the face wasn't the direct cause of death, so the crime was inflicting bodily injury. She collected signatures for me, some parents wrote petitions asking for leniency, and the lawyer said I should hold out until we could get a verdict of not guilty. But when they offered probation, I thought, *Okay, that's enough.* I quit my job as a teacher, too."

"What're you going to do now?"

"I haven't decided yet. I'd like to take time to consider things, including how my life would have turned out if that murder had never happened. I'm worried about the other two, also."

"It's going to take more time for them."

"Self-defense and insanity. Those are hard to prove. But they did turn themselves in and didn't have intent to kill. And they have well-known lawyers defending them, so I think it'll work out. I'm hopeful, at least. But who knows."

"They'll do what their lawyers tell them to, so I think it'll turn out okay. But you know—I was kind of surprised that you had her find a lawyer for you."

"You thought I'd turn her down?"

"If it had been me, I would have."

"It's like...I just decided to go ahead and accept her good intentions. I realized how powerless I was and gave up clinging to any stupid pride. And your case—I couldn't believe you got it reduced to an accident. It seemed like you were going to admit you'd pushed him down, even though you didn't have to. Just to get back at her."

"Because it's not just me anymore. I'm a single mother, and it would be hard on my child to have a criminal for a mother."

"I see. You've really matured, haven't you."

"Actually, I think I can understand her feelings at the time Emily was killed. If I were in her shoes, I might have said the same sort of thing to the kids she was playing with."

"Mothers are scary. Or *tough*, maybe? You're living with your parents, right? How many years will it be until your child is going to this school?"

"Didn't you hear? Next March they're going to close the school. Declining birth rates. The kids in this town will commute by school bus to the next town over. The school buildings are old, too, and they're going to tear the whole place down."

"That's why you got in touch with me?"

"Sorry. And you said all four of us should get together."

"No, it's okay. I'm glad I could come here before it's gone....Let's put an end to it, the two of us."

"Right. It's all over.... Before long I imagine this town will be incorporated into another and the town itself will no longer exist."

"It's too bad. I mean, since it's got the cleanest air in Japan."

"The clean air will still be here."

The two of them smiled at each other.

"Greensleeves" started to play quietly.

"Shall we go?"

They stood up.

And looked at the small bouquet.

"It's like that cake that time."

"You're right. I asked the florist to make up a bouquet that a ten-year-old girl would enjoy."

Find the murderer before the statute of limitations is up. If you can't do that, then atone for what you've done, in a way I'll accept.

The two walked toward the pool.

"Let's pray for Emily. Why didn't we realize that back then? The one thing we should have done the most?"

"Maybe we needed these fifteen years to finally understand."

Their shadows lengthen along the playground.

And twilight envelops the small town.

ABOUT THE AUTHOR

Kanae Minato is an internationally bestselling novelist and former home economics teacher and housewife who wrote her first novel, *Confessions*, between household chores. *Confessions* won several literary awards, including the Radio Drama Award, the Detective Novel Prize for New Writers, and the National Booksellers' Award, and was adapted into an Academy Award–nominated film directed by Tetsuya Nakashima. Minato lives in Japan.

ABOUT THE TRANSLATOR

Philip Gabriel is a professor of Japanese literature in the Department of East Asian Studies at the University of Arizona. His translations include many novels and short stories by the writer Haruki Murakami, most recently *Colorless Tsukuru Tazaki and His Years of Pilgrimage*. Gabriel received the Japan–U.S. Friendship Commission Prize for the Translation of Japanese Literature for his translation of Senji Kuroi's *Life in the Cul-de-Sac*, and the PEN/Book-of-the-Month Club Translation Prize for his translation of Murakami's *Kafka on the Shore*.

MULHOLLAND BOOKS

You won't be able to put down these Mulholland books.

....

....

Visit mulhollandbooks.com for
your daily suspense fix.